THE EYE OF THE CHILD

THE EYE OF THE CHILD

by RUTH MUELLER

new society publishers

Inquiries regarding requests to republish all or part of *The Eye of the Child* should be addressed to New Society Publishers, 4722 Baltimore Avenue, Philadelphia, PA 19143.
ISBN: 0-86571-046-5 Hardbound
      0-86571-039-2 Paperbound
Printed in the United States
Cover design by David Willoughby
Book design by Nina Huizinga

New Society Publishers is a project of New Society Educational Foundation and a collective of Movement for a New Society. New Society Educational Foundation is a nonprofit, tax-exempt foundation. Tax deductible contributions can be made to any of their projects by writing to New Society Educational Foundation, 4722 Baltimore Avenue, Philadelphia, PA 19143. Movement for a New Society is a network of small groups and individuals working for fundamental social change through nonviolent action. To learn more about MNS, write: Movement for a New Society, 4722 Baltimore Avenue, Philadelphia, PA 19143.

FOR
NANCY AND BILL
AND
ALL THE OTHERS

BOOK ONE

BY
MINI

INTRODUCTION

Where is that dawn garden now? Clothed in this myth or that where is that lost place of all our beginnings when we were still a part of and not apart from all that is? Once creatures among creatures, where now is that timeplace of primal awakening when animal innocence was shattered by the knowledge of good and of evil, that separating godlike knowing that rendered kind distinct, apart, cast out into reason and reasons?

Has mercy deceived us? Is the myth in whatever guise but cover for the truth of the cave, the brutish beginning? Unfinished, incomplete, still in the process, still painfully feeling the pulse of *what is* within spiral hope, do we yearn for something we have never yet known?

Return. Some say. Return sweet native. Return where? To the past? Or return to the future? Return to the cave? Or return to a new plateau again restored to oneness? Return—this time with a difference. This time with knowing but a knowing purged in trial and change, an awareness home from separation, from disunity with source.

5

Of one thing be sure. The garden is real. With or without us. Something lost. Or yet to be gained. Then. Now. A place out of shadow and light but as factual as tissue and soil. Radiating the animate because it is animate with a prescience tuned finer than knowing as of a lowly companion at one with each one in the midst of its own routine glory. But not waiting. Moving. Forever moving. Wait! How can one synchronize self with worlds within worlds before worlds beyond worlds?

In this there is hope. The eye of the child has seen the stunning fact of grasses and stars, and ear, in spite of all din has heard a whisper too subtle for words—

> *The gods of the land and the goddesses of the land*
> *have betaken themselves to sleep in heaven.*
> *They are not pronouncing judgment;*
> *they are not deciding things.*
> *Veiled is the night;*
> *the temple and the most holy places are quiet and*
> *   dark.*
> *The traveler calls on his god.**

*Cuneiform inscription on clay tablet, circa 3000 B.C.

6

ONE

WORLDHOVERINGWINGSING

I don't know when it first came to me that I could speak bird. From the beginning I never underestimated this strange thing or allowed it to slip down into a delusion. How to convince others, of course, would be a problem. I could appreciate how they might react. Science claims, it's a well-known fact, that nothing can ever happen for the first time. Why? Because it has always happened before. A second time, why not. But never, be reasonable, a first. Yet here we were with a first as bold as a jay. How, then, should I handle it?

Then it came to me. Why make a problem of it by trying to convince people? Whether they believed or not was beside the point. I would simply go ahead without a world-jolting science-rocking claim. If a nuthatch or titmouse or chickadee spoke to me I would speak back. Quietly. Without fanfare. If in turn someone noticed and made a thing of it, I would handle the incident as it came up, happening by happening.

But if no one should notice?

So? The birds and I would have a secret as high and open as noon, a thing as bright and uncontained as sun and chimes, seemingly hidden yet as unconcealed as the kiss of day on the forehead of the blind. What a thing. To see what even the seeing can't see. To hear what even the hearing can't hear. O! Why me, Mini singled out this way? But how long—how long?—would we, the birds and I, be able to contain anything so—so— *omnibracing*?

* * *

Daffy's coming had been entirely unspectacular. I first encountered her while taking up the yin feed to the flyway high feeders on top of our updated ziggurat. She simply appeared among a gaggle of pigeons at feeding time but looked different from any of them. Pecking at the millet with almost the same neck gesture as the others it came to me in a flash what the difference was between a dove and a pigeon: as distinct from a pigeon, even a fancy pigeon, a dove has the look of a person about her.

Please get this thing clear. In speaking of this—this— *look*—I don't mean to say a dove has anything like human features. She's as much bird as anybody. What I really mean is when she looks at you you know you've been looked at. Her stare is like someone you know but can't name.

Aside from which, naturally, she was more slender

with a melting neck line as tender as dawn flight, her color sun-snow bright.

"Daffodil!"

That is what I called her for no reason except that when I first saw her in all her sudden doveness, my tongue tripped into joy hinged non sense. Also, in the same flash, the fact that the first peace children, my little mother among them, carried daffodils way back then beg, beg, begging to blot out the heartbreak war and in return look, look, looking for a human look—one long sure look—to say "Another way! Another way!"

Actually Daffodil's own (born) name was something far out and wing-singing strange, plus totally world hovering, expressed in one flowing blended singsong syllable. This was because when rendered into human it came out far east, natural to her because she was born (hatched, actually) in a temple dovecote so far east it stands where the day itself is born.

"As for the four directions," I told her by way of welcome, "I love East best of all. Beginnings, you know. Of course South is nice too. Fun in The Garden. But I suppose we shouldn't put down old North and West. At least, globewise, they hold things together, rock and ice being more everywhere than glue in nature's scheme. For the big scene, magnetic is better than sticky. Right?"

"Right," she confirmed, returning to the millet.

"Your name translates into Daffodil," I storied. "Do you mind?"

It was then she turned and gave me The Look.

11

"It translates into Worldhoveringwingsing,"* she corrected.

"How will I get around all that?"

"Call me Daffy or even Dilly if it's more at home for your everyday tongue," she conceded, apparently unconcerned with anything except pecking up her supper after a long flight.

"How is peace coming along?" I asked.

"Please! I'm eating!"

She gave a weary little flutter but failed even to look up.

It was then I was hit with a heavy thought. Of course it must be true. Like all the rest of us a dove must be mortal. She could die? *Or even get too tired to care?*

In the fragile moment after the pigeons had flocked off and she was left alone, replete and making little preening gestures, I intruded with no further word. I held silence too when, in the thickening dusk, she flew to the summit railing and, standing on one foot, tucked her head under her wing and went to sleep.

All through the night, fitfully dozing, I woke at intervals to check on the still-standing, slightly puffed up strange little profile against the dark but luminous sky. Then at dawn—O me!—I woke suddenly out of a turbulent but fading dream to find her gone. The railing was edged sharp but empty against the first faint feelers of the coming day. I ran to the place where she had been but the only sign of her I could find was one footprint in

*See calligraphy, opposite

巧

翅

13

the not quite dry cement we had used the day before to mend a crumbling spot.

"Daffodil! Why? Why?"

Without think almost by reflex, out of some urge to recall and retrieve I found myself pointedly but carefully tracing a circle around the small clear doveprint on the railing.

For one moment I did not realize what was staring back up at me.

Not an eye.

Not really.

But a LOOKING thing. Like sight itself focusing sudden awareness. Emerged full and etched keen. Yes. It was true. Swimming up out of my dreaming and focusing now out of clear waking, delicate but definite in the new cement—a glip.

A live glip?

So. At least a glip made by a live dove. The real imprint of the real. A primal. But more. A special primal. One of a kind. One of an *only* kind?

For a moment I stared, trying to take in all the dimensions.

What if it was her? Herself? *The one?*

A glip of the world, then?

At the very least!

There in the dim dawn light, within reach, touchable, shining up out of the morning dew and ringed by the universal circle I had unconsciously added, the doveprint on the railing loomed up this way

Worldhoveringwingsing! Come back! Come back!

TWO

THE STOOP

Not every arrival can be unspectacular.

It was on an entirely different day, in fact the next one, when I suddenly remembered with vivid vibrations what the dream was I had been dreaming just before I woke to find the dove gone. How shall I say it? Sitting high on the same summit terrace and waiting with the feeders full for the birds who—strangely—never came, I saw day itself turn angry, rolling up in a kind of premature night from all directions, the far clear horizon but a moment before showing sharp slate-blue against a luminous grey line, now blurred all around the edge with suddenly gathered in-rolling cloud banks, turbulent black purplish as of some cosmic cauldron boiling over from below the surface all around the rim of the world.

Why was I sad instead of afraid? Who was I crying for? For ourselves? For the missing birds who seemed to have deserted? For the blue gone out of the sky? *Forever*?

What color is grief for a spoiled creation? When creation itself erupts to cry?

Seth! Seth! Seth! Why was he so long in returning?

But quiet. It was only a dream. True, now I was once again sky high on top waiting with filled feeders, but this day was not that kind of day. The sun was shining, thin, with thin blue still showing through the high thin chronic haze. Shading my eyes and blinking straight up into reality's huge, in fact infinite dome, did I imagine that just for one second the sun, in turn, blinked? Not *out*. But like a near and massive star twink.

What could have caused such a thing? A body of some sort momentarily passing between my line of vision and the source of our light and warmth?

What sort of body would be way up there solid enough to create the illusion of a solar twink? A flying saucer from an advanced group farther out in time and space come to save us from our self-inflicted fate? Provided they didn't get shot down on landing of course—or worse— inadvertently trip any one of the multiple nation alarm systems to start The Big One. WARNING. All you creatures out there in space, caution on approach. Our gorgeous sweet-looking big blue planet is one big self-triggered cosmic bomb.

So? If not would-be saviors or others from space, then some entity from still farther out? A defiantly opaque ghost, for example, kinkily acting out for kicks? Or, closer in a more mundane if fatal groove, a normally befouling ozone-nipping supersonic jet with its engine gone silently dead and ready to take the final plunge?

Or, relax, none of these. But a bird. A big bird.

Of course a bird. But what big bird?

I knew of course. The prideful showoff winking of the

20

sun, that alone would give him away, the grand manipulator, the greatest thing on wings. For speed. For stamina. For outright killing power.

To put it another way, do you know what *one fell swoop* means?

It means Harry is on the way down at up to 200 miles per hour, splitting air straight open from up. Way up. So far up he starts as less than a speck. But grows. Explosively. A unique materialization from out of nothing into a solid striking something. It means a sleek live body, bullet aimed, hurtling downward through space in a blurred streak faster than the eye can trace, yet hawkeye centered on target, talon sharp for the gut-bloody spine-crunching single stroke kill.

The original dive bomber.

Zoop! Up he goes in reverse arc without even touching ground, slowed only slightly by the burden of the broken corpse in his clutch. Flap. Flap. A mere cargo plane now. Over the ridge to enjoy the spoils or to share with Junior and his beaky old dear.

A baby rabbit? A ground hog? A hapless wild duck? A panicked young chicken strayed out of the coop?

No struggle. No struggle at all. One moment a furry or feathered warm body minding its business. The next a demise so sudden and total it must be almost painless.

On the other hand I suppose you'd hardly call it Operation Mercy.

But what about now? This moment? Did he have us in his sights? If so, what for? Not for millet, cracked corn and sunflower seed. He would only scoff at such fare.

Once more I stared up into the celestial vault, my eyes smarting, seeing nothing but a blurr of light and haze. The dulcid clucking of Amarella our neighbor hen on the sixth level just below, brought me back with a zeroed-in ping: *a current of slow electricity began to race along my spine—*

Of course. The hen and her little brood including new Chérie, the tiny fluff bit-of-life who had cracked her natal egg today. Yes. Chérie, the yellow fuzz epitome of baby chickenhood, already *cheep, cheep, cheeping* with a built-in if-one-word vocabulary to signal that she, too, had come—

No. Never. No! Not after all those millions of years of evolution just to arrive at this one moment (plus, don't forget the extra 21 days inside the egg), working, striving, pulsating in harmony with the master plan, growing cell by cell in blind expectation toward the great moment, the heroic, the brave no turning back struggle of The Big Crack Out—

—with a wee animate masterpiece.

The crowning goal of the whole tremendous process—

—peeping on her own—

No. *Never*—

As I jumped up I felt the enveloping downrush before actually hearing it, pointed silence itself a leading nose-cone for a trailing shirring—what?

"Amarella! C–H–É–R–I–E—"

Was someone screaming? *Me?*

To the sound of exploded cackling from the level just below I hit the pile of sand beside the summit rain pool, prone, not out of fear but merely responding to normal panic, a reality response to a reality situation.

So *that's* the way the clever badger burrows under in such a hurry.

*   *   *

My spine crawled. My scalp tingled. Not so much with the prickling inrush of loose sand as with a sticking sense of being pinpointed at the nadir of a vortex—

—I felt the ws–o–oo–s–h—

—the glancing crease of a whirlwind muffled through the sand, with a sudden whipping reverberation in reverse. Then silence itself swiftly rising. The uprise. The famous uprise. With wings, no doubt, bloomed out whole and wide. The swift but effortless reverse mount almost straight up on a self-created jet of unspent momentum and air—

Master of wings!
Bird of steely beauty and fright
Of flight
Of far far burning yellow sight
Of bloody claw—

I strained to hear what was no longer there. Silence was now blooming out whole and wide like a vast sheltering parachute descending; air poured back into the funneled void and I started to breathe again—

— —

At last.

— —

It was all over.

23

* * *

I raised one shoulder out of the sand, blinking. I listened in a vacuum. Had Amarella made it? Had the hysterics-prone but brave old creature once more risen to the occasion, making it to the far side of the defunct museum-piece-old chopping block for shelter with her little ones? Then it came. The faint sounds of re-emerging life on the sixth level, tentative indignant clucking and the half-smothered peeping of the babies as they struggled out from under their mother's copious feathered bottom.

"Chérie," I called, my mouth full of sand.

"Cheep."

THREE
THE CAGE

Was it, in this case, a going instead of a coming?

He was winged night, captured and caged. He was the pulse of the forest snared and then reduced to a flapping shadow among deeper shadows with no shaft of light on the subject except what flashed from angry eyes. Sitting momentarily quiet in ruffled exhaustion when I came upon him, his rotund bulk loomed up as a blurred but vibrating field of dejection within the thickening dark.

"Orison?"

I stood before the circular metal fence topped with its mesh canopy, high and roomy by people standards but low and cramped for even one small full-winged sweep, and I knew I was going to break the law. Plus the lock. In fact both together. On behalf of higher law of course. So? Here once again was the running conflict of "law" against law with the answer this time as bright and beckoning as a star path across night water.

Is there any law that is a real law unless it is in harmony with the health of being, with—in fact—the way of life itself? If a bird has wings he is meant to fly by a decree built in by life itself. To put him in a position where that built-in decree is broken is to break the law of wings, a crime not only against the creature but against that which evolved winging.

"The Law of Locks vs. the Law of Wings?"

No choice was necessary because the choice had already been made the minute I saw him. Even so should I not try channels first? Give them one more chance, the lock people? Down here in The Sprawl where the old ways were still bedded in, should I not try the top zoo boss, going either alone by one or in a group of two or three or more for support, with or without signs, a human-to-human encounter in flat-out peace, asking for the great bird's release on the sheer merits of the case or—if that didn't work—falling back on a statement of animal rights?

How forlorn a cause can you get? With guaranteed defeat built in. Sincere appeal reduced to a gesture, a meaningless ritual hoping for a miracle change of consciousness. No. If they still locked up people in cages who was going to worry about a "mere" bird? If people still had their life-authored rights trampled who would do anything but laugh at the idea of animal rights?

Why could I never get it across? Not with bird calls. But direct. Plain. Simple. With human words in their own language. To say as clear as clear water is clear: IT IS ALL ONE FRONT, IT IS ALL ONE FRONT, IT IS ALL ONE FRONT *against what life does not intend*—

Where was even a flicker of hope? Among other things they had already paid out money for him and received his live bulk in return. The binding green stuff had passed,

28

the sacred if ersatz wampum: THE GREATEST SPEC-
IMEN IN CAPTIVITY the sign over the cage said in big
letters still smelling of fresh gilt.

"Orison?" I said his name through the bars, clear but
soft.

Was he facing forward or standing with his back toward me? I peered. It was hard to tell in the dim light.
In one way it seemed sure that he was fronting forward.
The feathered expanse of his stomach with claws clutch-
ing on the big perch bar were both heading toward me
but, even so, can you say that a bird or any other creature
is facing you when his face as such is facing to the rear?
Where there is even a striking impression of his head
being set on backward?

I had seen his gesture of turning away as I came closer,
a gesture accomplished not by turning his body but merely
by rotating his head as if he had a level pivot where his
neck should be. Now the big blank back of his head with
twin ear tufts standing at reverse attention presented a
rebuffing non-front that topped his stomach without ben-
efit of any visible neck, the whole blind stance an elo-
quent non-verbal shut-out of total proportions.

"Orison!" I called more urgently.

Well. There was more than one way around a problem.
I tried walking around the big cage, a hexagonal thing
edged with cindery flower beds and six benches, one on
each of the hex sides for people to sit on and stare at him
at leisure while resting their feet. A living symbol of Dignity and Mystery is how the zoo blurb described him.
Dignity? Mystery? How could either be maintained even

29

by one of such prodigious natural dignity with all his secrets plucked and exposed in close stinking confinement? Where there were encircling crowds how would he ever get away by the mere swiveling of his head? Then there would be laughs. Spreading laughs turning uproarious. With pointing. Even hoots? But now, just as I seemed gaining on turning the sixth and final corner onto his face, my only reward was to have him snap his head back to where I no longer was.

"Orison," I tried again, "I'm going to get you out."

How? I had no real idea but of one thing I was sure. If there was a way to get him into that cage there was, in reverse, a way out. It was a matter of shrewdie reverse logic plus plugged in can-do. The kind of go that is not going to be stopped by mere ignorance or other such flak. Of course it would call for at least some technological knowhow in the field of zoo springing. So okay. It might not be all that easy. There would be any number of things needed. But they could all be rapped out and acted out with willing helpers. Plus a blow torch? Or a bobby pin?

I stood grasping two of the bars, my face pressed against the metal, waiting, refusing to leave. Even if he won't pay attention I'll help him I told myself.

I wasn't prepared for what happened next.

With no warning, in the blink of a flick, his head snapped around again and by his tipping his body at an angle on the perch I was projected full into the unblinking middle of his sights. What a wild zoom! Have you ever seen yourself reflected in twin owl beams? Seen the real you multiplied by two and glowing darkly in living

30

black pools framed by angry yellow? I stared back and then grasped the bars for support: the coagulating nocturnal distress cry of *Strigiform Bubo virginianus virginianus* rent the flaccid ambiance that passes for air over The Sprawl, rent it as a limp sheet zigzagged to curled and smoking shreds in a Stygian lightening strike—

O!

Heard from a decent distance in a forest at night such a cry has been known to bring hapless sleepers up standing inside their sleeping bags, dazed, armed with nothing but their inner juices and ready to face the final test—

O!

Heard freeze dry from a few feet away the ears become hollow channels of the furies, the head an echo chamber for the haunts with minds blown feather weight and scattered as down in a whistling wind. How shall the stricken strike! Cry of the world! Of all distress trapped and hanging by a bloody string! O! Why did not people, too, have such a cry to cry out so all the world could hear?

My knees were floating, my hands bit in on metal for support, my tongue found syllables that stumbled into words, "We're coming— We're coming—" Even my shaking, while total, was weak. "Hold on. Hold on. You'll soon be free."

So.

I had made a promise and he had pounced on it. Now the deed was our only way out.

To free us as well as him.

FOUR
THE PLACE

Was he the real Orison?

Did it matter?

But yes. In that wild zoom had there not been a spark of recognition?

How long had it been since I had been to The Place Where All Things Come Together? Way back then I had been as much a new human as he had been a new owlet. Fallen out of his nest and half dead. It isn't easy to become a mother at age six but that's what I became to him, a mother owl.

"Run—run—" my father had said, "to The Place—"

We had been there often in the green world, our place of recurring return, our center within the larger circling domain where no soil was alien and home was wherever we were. In that place sun dappled down in a way no other familiar in creation is capable of doing, provided it has a live forest to dapple in. Starting at 90,000,000 (million) miles out in space single rays travelled all that way to settle on single cells on single leaves, reflecting glossy light and piercing with translucent passion to set off a mad dance in the inner juices, an affinity deeper than love. A million leaves sparkling between light and shade as wisps and breezes caught in the singing combs of a thousand branches breathing with the whole earth, a part, not apart, close and here and now where everything comes together.

True, no one place is any more *here* than any other but, for you, only the locale where you are at the time. But this was a place I could think myself into as well as go to, a real place that was always brighter than a dream. It was inner space come to life in the touchable, the tangible at the bottom of an ocean of swaying green light, breathable with the fragrance of damp earth and of plant breath exhaled. It was air sparkling and then melting between flashes of gold and velvet shafts of shade, the solid trunks, the massive stems of giant plants, crown high, huge and towering. The old rare oaks had dried-out alligator hide for bark, grooved brown and ridged rough and deep. The beeches, smooth and soaring grey, had frozen elephant hide for skin. And don't forget the great wild cherry, friend of waxwing and jay. They had midnight-colored skin like huge harmless serpents at molting time.

Who told me all that?

My father sang whenever he burst upon the sea. Sang with shouting loud to the wind, sometimes with me on his shoulders and my hair flying and my arms out cutting the wind like a bird. He held my ankles in a grip of safety on his chest and ran barefoot through the sand and I flew with no fear of falling. But this was not our open place at the sea. This was our inner place. The green world, not the blue and yellow. I loved them both, dear familiars, dawn gardens. But in the green was shelter, the right to hide when hide you must.

That was it. That's what he meant, "Run, run," he said, "to The Place—" I must hide, this time alone. I caught my breath. Until they came. Only until they came—

"Home is where we are," my mother said the last time I ever saw her, "home we take with us. Remember? We are never lost."

How was I to know then that when my parents sent me to hide in our place in the forest they were trying to protect me? Traveling street mimes, intentional fools, jesters to the world, Mox and Tranquilli were being hassled by the authorities to put their child, me, in school in accord with the law, either by settling down in one place with what was called a useful job or, failing that, at least to go on welfare like countable settled folk. Or worse, if we insisted on continuing our roving "nonproductive" lifestyle, to surrender "the child" for foster placement.

"Over my dead body," said Tranquilli.

"They'd have to lock me up first, " said Mox. "and throw away the key."

One step ahead of a charge of child neglect or exploitation (done up like a raggedy doll with my own orange hair and candy–stripe hose I passed the hat as well as performed), there was danger they would be declared unfit and I made a ward of The State. Hence the extreme step, pending—who knows what? For the present, at least, if no child was there no child could be taken away. Right?

Fear at first didn't figure. I was going to our place where the night, like day, was benign, where every bush and turn in the path held pulses of happy times. Also, above all, there was the abiding fact that I was The One Who Would Never Be Abandoned. Hadn't my mother herself told me that not once but many times? "Mini always remember this. You were the one who was born so you could know what it is never to be abandoned." Okay. Okay. So I didn't want to hear it all over again. Mox with one hand on her forehead to pour in strength, the other hand under her spine to draw off the pain. The new one naturally a little one. A tender one. But absolutely certain from the very beginning. Under the arms, the sheltering arms, helpless but slung in a lovin' sling, under her breasts or over his back, the feel and the good warm scent of my parents' bodies, yes, yes, yes, as primal as earth, as true, as real.

"Remember," shouted Mox as I started off with my backpack of provisions scaled to size, "you're the most powerful six-year-old in the entire world! Powerful! Powerful!"

* * *

How thankful I was that my parents had this habit of scattering seeds wherever we went because, as I came into the sunny clearing, there was a glory apple, a lush tomato, glowing dark red, so ripe it almost fell into my hand as if waiting just for me. A welcome sign, a good omen. Of course our rite of scattering seeds as we moved out into any new place, didn't always turn out so well. Dried sunflower and other flower seeds, tree pods and nuts, fruit pits, all kinds of food seeds saved for this purpose, some fell on concrete streets or hardtop roads and could not take root. What would you expect? They were crushed under walking feet or rolling tires unless pecked up first by hungry city birds, mostly flocks of sparrows or pigeons. Others fell on the shoulders of highways, on packed dirt or cinders. Some of these hopefully showed shoots only to be mowed down by the road crews whose job it was to treat even a rare lily like a "weed" if it was growing in the wrong place. The same fate happened to others that fell into clipped lawns. They too were cut down at intervals and artificially stunted because conditions wouldn't let them grow more than an inch or two no matter how hard they tried. The uniform lawn grass had adapted and could take it but the exceptional plants finally withered and died—if they were not targeted first by a nasty blast of herbicide meant just for them. Some seeds were lost in other ways like those landing down a drain pipe where they could not get their share of light and where sooner or later they rotted from the inside out. Except for crippled tries, these produced no yield. Others, though—and this is what saved the whole thing from being a total down pass—others fell into loam, good ground with light, air and rain all working with and in and through them, and these sprang up and grew into the fullness of what they were meant to be.

Like the glory fruit in my hand. Now, that first day,

as I stood at the spring I saw that there were other luscious glowing globes in the bright clearing, some red, yellow, green, big, little. The tiny onions, not in a row but pigglety in an exposed patch showed shoots near a damp bank of wild watercress. Beets and carrots, too, they were growing here and there like weeds, red and orange under the ground for the pulling. Joy in the morning! What was that big vine with the bright yellow blooms? A huge squash tangle rambling down the side of a sunny land fall. But the peanut bushes had hardly taken hold among the roses, now almost wild. There were snapdragons among the wayside tiger lilies and morning glory ground-crawling among Indian pipes and forest violets, new birch shoots both silk and silver, a peach pit seedling, two dwarf melons and here and there a stalk of stunted corn waving blond silk. Too much shade? Watch it! Was that a striped snake under that ground leaf? No. Merely a surprise zucchini. With a real-life little snake curled flat in its cuddle curve, its glossy scales as clean as a coil-woven round placemat, a funny little marvel asleep in creature peace.

But my poor baby! Sweeter than any doll and trembling with life. An owlet, gaping, fragile, grounded, making little *click* sounds with his beak. Abandoned by his own? I chewed up nuts and fed them down his gullet, swallowing some for myself. I wanted to cuddle him but he didn't go for that. His sharp little beak pecked at me during a trial squeeze, not to hurt but to draw the limits. That was the thing. Orison wouldn't hurt his make-do better-than-nothing mother but he did—even then—lay out the limits.

When would they come?

Day after day, how long did it go on? Was it the first night or later that I had the dream, dark in a lost strange place, a wide saucer of land abandoned by people and floored only by the stone foot marks of those terrible vanished dragons, once real, no fairy tale, who had lived and ruled our planet before people were people. In the midst of it there was a wavering that towered and beckoned like a living presence: *go there*. I heard her voice. Tranquilli's. So real, so near I leaped awake. Her tone was usual but crystalline insistent like ringing glass. A voice held steady not to frighten but to impel beyond fear. I answered no. I was in The Place Where All Things Come Together, our place where they themselves had sent me. I knew what to do. I was to remain until they came. No! Dreams were sometimes crazy. Tranquilli herself said so. I would trust my recall of their waking voices. Besides they would never beckon me to a place that was itself lost. As for the dragons, we had already settled their hash. By making an act of them. In the end, I remembered one was reduced to the size of a bird on my father's head and he took wing and flew away.

How long did it go on? No. There was another reason why I could not leave even if I could leave. The owl. I would not abandon him as long as he needed me but in the meantime where was my mother, my father? Old Hera was great of course, ever present, never leaving,

41

and I could lie on her breast in the sun for comfort. But why with all its singing did the wind form no actual word? Because if it spoke my way it would then have to cry out in all those others, el Español or Onondaga or Whatever from Where? *All* of them? The whole windy bag as big as the world blended together and sounding, anyway, like nothing except a wind? Could that be what a wind was? The voice of everyone together, saying something, trying to be heard? Why didn't the baby get on with flying, with striking out for himself?

Striking?

Had I said *striking*?

I shivered.

What about the vole in the moonlight?

How could I forget her?

Had it been the first night or the second? I had been sitting hugging myself, rocking and crying soundlessly in the still silver light. Then I saw it. Close enough to touch. A bit of movement on a rock as bright as a chunk of moon fallen and glowing on its own, a creeping shadow, congealing into a tiny spot and taking form. No bigger than a newborn mouse, the minute creature seemed to pull itself together to sit trembling in the center of the rock, two pin-point gleams of light shining where its eyes must be. Could it see me? I quit breathing, quit rocking, I tensed still as the rock, without sound, without movement.

Could it be a little person? First he seemed to draw himself up to make a speech, then she seemed to be poised to take a ballet step. But no, the little thing couldn't be human. Its ears were too big for the rest of it and set on its head at the wrong angle. No. It was a vole. Just a vole. Vole, little person, hello. Could it hear my thoughts? I won't hurt you, Voletta dear. Never fear.

Was its burrow under the rock? A night creature like the owl, had it come out for fresh air or just to stretch in the moon? My dried tears tasted salty on my cheeks and we sat motionless, looking at each other. Waiting on who would move first? At last I put one hand out, not to touch but to cup a shadow umbrella above the little thing as a sort of open greeting. In that moment she was gone. A vanishing. Like magic. Well—that made sense. Such a little weakie. What protection did she have against all the night prowlers and pouncers except such disappearing magic? Nature always provides all her creatures with some kind of help and in the vole's case it was nervous quickness. To be quick was to be alive.

Dear little vole I don't pounce to crush, to eat. You could even sit on my hand. Come back, Voletta, we could be friends.

So? That was all for that night. But the next? Would she come back tomorrow night, little sister? Yes, now I was sure she was she. Otherwise how could I have a little sister?

I sprinkled wild seed on the rock and waited, sleepy, not crying, arms locked around knees to hold steady. Out of a dream I opened my eyes to find her there, munching, visibly growing fat on the spread before my eyes. I waited, I whispered like a breeze, she tensed and stared but did not move. Gently, gently, as silent as a cloud I put out a hand. In that instant she was gone but this time I saw her go, a moving streak. Had she hesitated just a little, enough for eye to follow?

That's how it started, the night visits of the vole. By the forth night baby Orison was restless in the background, chittering and fluttering his wings, stretching, head and body tipped forward as if to spy. Was he going to fly at last?

Then it came to me. Something I had known all along, something I had put down. Now it was up and open and staring me in the face. If he was to survive, if he was to grow up to his full, Orison would have to do more than merely fly.

Strike?

No more nut mash, grubs, scrounged pieces of earthworm.

I shivered.

It was time for me to go. Into a pitched corner of panic, stumbling, half seeing. My own, my own were terribly lost. That now was clear as a shattered secret is clear after exposure. Why had I waited so long? I must not only go, I must run with no looking back. Orison can manage too well! But no. The vole? How could I warn the vole? At the coming of the last dusk Orison had swooped. He was airborne at last. But could he steer for a telling strike? I swept all the seeds off the rock. I kicked it. I made it tremble. Fair warning! But the test would still come—would come—and the vole was half tame, half trusting—

I must go. Tear loose. I must run as I'd never run before. Through brambles, around stumps, over the moss-covered trunks of fallen giants. In the early light of a new day my own were lost. I knew the truth now. They were not coming back for me. Somehow, some way, my own were terribly, terribly lost.

FIVE

THE SPRINGING

How to free the owl?

At Mount Heapmore that was the problem tossed into the middle of everything for all who came to the council circle in the ground-level world room. As problem presenter I pointed out, "There are two ways to meet this thing of freeing the owl. The first would be to build a cage as big as Rhode Island and set it down in the middle of New Jersey so he could flap around inside with an illusion of being free. Or two: turn him loose really free. Total. The only limit the planet's envelope of breathable vapor. In the number two case, unlike so-called number one, he could disappear at will, his own bird, free not only for himself but from us. Above all he wouldn't have to just sit there like now while people ringed him to watch him suffer."

The response was spontaneous. It was number two all the way. The question, in fact, was never whether but how? Here the problem took on sticky dimensions. How do you get an owl out of a cage as tight as a prison cell clanged shut and in a vague sort of way guarded?

The suggestions from around the circle varied all the way from here to there and back again with some of the children even getting a spot for their say. Remember, if given a chance, new humans sometimes see straight into instead of all around and who knows where a kernel will sprout? In the end the heaviest of the ideas jelled into a seven-point list for a closer look pending an outcome, as follows:

1. Pick the lock at an off hour, meaning better at night when the nocturnal bird is alert and the diurnal guard is not?

2. Be more open and heroic about it. Declare war and blast the lock (if necessary the whole cage) in courageous combative defiance with an armed attack in open daylight, prepared to shed blood, God forbid, if necessary, in offensive defense of the fundamental universal issue at stake?

3. Be realistic. Work from where you are with what you've got. In short negotiate from a position of weakness.

Hold it!

Don't apologize. Weak from their viewpoint only. Remember that alternate mox in a different groove. Make an offer to replace Orison with a fair-exchange proxy? Would they, for example, by some crazy fluke, accept one of Farmer Merebalm's now famous woodcarvings to sit on the cage perch, an arty replica and future museum piece all in one? Plus—go overboard for good measure—offer a bonus: a spectacular planting of the well-fertilized dirt cage floor in brilliant blue hyacinths, brighter-than-white phlox and scarlet geraniums spelling out in living red, white and blue: FREE.

4. Resort to their own tactics vis-a-vis the wild ones? Lay in wait for the rare cage cleaning and when the door is opened shoot the attendant with a so-called harmless tranquilizer dart like the kind that is so-called harmlessly used on wild creatures to so-called harmlessly render them really harmless for everything from so-called beneficial lab data ear taggings to so-called benign capture?

5. Stick to nonviolence. Remember. Means are ends unfolding. Gather in a nonarmy to strategically surround the cage while sending a negotiating team forward to the zoo boss and all together, with sincere vibes, make one last appeal for animal rights, inviting the lock authorities to join the cause. In the meantime, as a backup precaution, no one moves from around the cage unless taken bodily, in which case all go limp. Stick to your nonguns. Even if they lock you up.

6. Levitation? Far out? So? Mass psychokinetics? If that sister in Russia can move that world-famous toothpick a tweek of a millimeter even if, granted, with exhausting mental effort, what would happen if our whole community were to surround the cage and have a go at mentally moving the thing off its base? Or at least tweeking open the door?

7. Seven. A sweet number. For our seven levels? With decisions from the ground up and celebrations for all on top. What shall we say for number seven? A PRO-PERSONNEL BALM? What else? Meaning, naturally,

the exact diametrically opposed opposite of an anti-personnel bomb.

*　*　*

It was settled. With lookouts posted and diversionary flams planned, we sprung Orison in the dark of the moon to accommodate to his nocturnal ways; also so we could avoid drawing a counterforce against our nonforce as we made our move.

An outdated Rich-O-Matic credit card found discarded in a Sprawl alley trash can and slipped into the tired rusty old cage lock had not yielded the easy result hoped for. Dashed but still determined we next moved the council circle out around the cage at the zoo for onspot inperson whole vibe openings, soundlessly circling the cage with people as the bird stirred on his perch, alert. What was up? As our eyes became adjusted to the darkness I could see he was swiveling his head first this way, then that. "Orison, we've come to get you out," I hiss-whispered. The night fragrance of the park engulfed us like an embrace, an invitation, an enticement. The guard, we were assured, had already passed out of sight on his midnight punch-clock patrol. Someone gave a low whistle and, like me, was shushed for breaking our disciplined silence.

"If nothing happens tonight," signed Luz Marina, "don't get discouraged. We'll be back."

Now we were all around the cage, just sitting there on the ground with not so much as a twig snapped in the deployment. "It stands to reason," Sortie, an ex-war bomber turned dead serious peace balmer, was the first to come to grips with logistics, writing his words on a chalkboard with luminous chalk, "we're not going to get anywhere tipping the thing off its base with six master bolts clamping it down. What we need to bring us up even with level gravity is six volunteers with six wrenches."

As it turned out there were three people who had brought wrenches and twenty-two volunteers to use them. "Six at the bolt heads are it," declared Sortie, forgetting to chalk talk. The wrenches with some squealing and protesting, worked. All except one. At this point Apple stepped forward with her special thing, winesap-delicious seed oil, fine not only for cooking and salad but as an all-purpose lubricant as well. Poured generously over the old bolt its rusted threads finally yielded after four people had strained their ventral abdominal muscles, guts that is, in turn.

"Now," signed Sortie, "the cage is just standing there held down by nothing—"

"—except the same planetary magnetic force that is holding us down," countered someone else.

"—the attraction of the total mass of the world—"

"That's all—"

"What we need is a giant to lift the whole thing off its base from above like the lid off a pan," offered Sallie, Sortie's partner in love and storm.

"A derrick from above?"

"A grounded tilt bar from below?"

"Too much commotion—"

"—bring the guard?"

"Injure the bird?"

53

"Objection. Machine-intensive—"

"Can't we get gravity to work for us without all this fuss and feathers?"

"Or equalize it?"

"Suspend—"

During all this I noticed that Luz Marina had been circling the cage as if on a private trip, her long skirt swirling, speaking with her hips in growing impatience. What was she trying to convey? At last she stepped up to the base line horizontal bar that connected all six sides and served as a foundation prop on the low cement facing that edged the cage floor. She hooked her fingers around it lightly as if testing, and then shrugged. "We've got it made," she signaled, "the thing is as light as a feather. You'll see—"

All the others there at first certainly did not see but continued to sit immobile on the ground if, now, with attention focused, open, expectant.

"I can lift it," Luz avowed, confident, speaking softly but aloud. "I can lift it," she repeated, "but not alone—"

*   *   *

That's how it was done, six people along each of the six sides, each one of the thirty six persons weighing whatever they weighed but all together weighing far more than a giant, far more than the big iron cage. Of course not everyone who wanted to volunteer could get a handhold on the foundation bar and was counted out in the countaround. But I was one of the lucky ones and if I'm claiming now that that big bulky thing, heavy enough to crush a person had it fallen to one side, flew up like a feather hovering free on a breeze, would I be believed? It was amazing, strange, like a suddenly activated miracle. But at the same time easy and natural as if a live current of strength were flowing through all of us together, the efforts of all blending as one in the upsurge. True there was an initial wrench, a muffled metallic click as Luz counted down to zero to signal go; a dusty *zing* smelling of age and rot, then our heave, a gap, the gap swinging wider, the base bar finally over our heads and balanced there in equilibrium, the huge cage aloft on our ring of hands.

A massed sigh went up, a happy moan, a stifled cheer from both those holding and those watching.

Our troubles were over? Actually not. The fact was that our solid wall of bodies formed a barrier as imprisoning to the now excited bird as his cage bars had been. It was Heyzoos who first recognized the problem and jumped away from his place in the lift line, opening a space for the bird to escape. "Come out wise old fool," he shouted, silence tossed to the wind, "hurry before the crack of day!"

Still the bird hesitated. Why? Was the opening too narrow a passage for half-paralyzed wings? The two people who had been alongside Heyzoos also stepped aside, widening the portal to freedom. "Orison," I cried, "go, go, go. It's no trap."

In the end, with the escape route wide open, it was Greatfeller, a huge cooperating raccoon whom we had rescued, paw crippled from an unspeakable leg-hold trap,

55

who waddle-hobbled into the breach to reassure the pop-eyed bird and to hassle him out to safety by frantically pawing the perch support.

If an owl can detect a moving dinner under a ground leaf in the dark at twenty paces with his infra-mysterious night sight, can he also detect a gap gaping open to freedom?

He can—and he did. Zwoo-oo-p! The sudden swirling and fanning of air was prodigious. Felt as a spiraling breeze, seen as a winged fact fleeing, it was uncannily unheard as the great bird slanted and swooped out in flight as eerily soundless as velvet on cloud, the layer of gossamer fuzz on the tips of his feathers guaranteeing flight as silent as silent night.

Another muffled cheer went up.

Staggering a bit on cramped wings at first—or was that his parting salute?—he was off, wings pumping, sailing, pumping, higher, gaining altitude, up! off! safe! Higher, dimmer, his shadowy shape melted into the darkness above the tree-muted park lights, off, off, now straight as a native returning toward faroff green belt rise and The Place Where All Things (still?) Come Together.

SIX

THE NAMING

Tranquilli took the name Tranquilli because it was a matter of life and death. She had a defect in a blood vessel near her heart like a flaw in a balloon and when anyone shouted at her *Tranquilli Tranquilli* she knew what they meant. Then she calmed down. Or tried.

"Big deal," she said, "who needs it?"

She had a special right to choose her own name, of course, because she was one of that select group who are abandoned at birth and thrown on the mercies of whatever civilization is extant at the moment. In her case she had been found in a trembling shoebox on the East side subway in the tunnel between Manhattan and the Bronx. A cold dying blue, barely peeping, she was turned in at the change booth at the next stop by a rescuer who was held a full day by the police under vague suspicion because he could speak only Spanish and was out of work to boot. Later Tranquilli adopted her savior as her father in absentia, giving his fleeting image the name Guillermo, the brave one. Considered unadoptable because of a congenital heart defect, Nona as she was known

59

then (short for Noname) disappeared from the last of a series of institutions and foster homes in her early teens, presumably a runaway with a passing street carnival.

By the time I got to know her after my birth as her one true child, The One Who Would Never Be Abandoned, she could balance on a beam but never stoop over. "Stoop over and you're asking for it," threatened a doctor out of her past. Too young myself to tie my own shoes, that's when I learned we had to tie her dance thongs for her forever.

It's easier to learn to tie someone else's shoes than your own. Did you know that? Because you're standing in front of them but back of yourself.

Forever. Did I say forever? What we should have said was for as long as she needs us.

Sandals she could slip into. Provided they were in the right place at the right time. Shoes, shoes, first out of the pack and lined up in reach. But better bare feet. Feeling old Hera underfoot, gritty and hot in summer or cool on grass after a shower. Beautiful are the feet of those— who have beautiful feet. On a mountain top or, for that matter, at sea level. On the outer banks, say, with the laughing gulls wheeling and screaming and the sandpipers darting among the tidal pools. There Tranquilli walked in water at the edge like a ballerina in tune with the rhythm of waves, but Mox and Mini raced on the hot sand like the wild ponies no longer there. No longer there, that is, except for a remnant herd, calmed down, tamed down, on Okracoke. Listen! Can you hear the ghosts of the wild ones snorting and neighing over that dune? Where now are the Judas nag of Nag's Head and the spirit lights on the sand crests and the sea soughing and crying and drowning cries? That's where they sprinkled her because that's where she wanted to be, the exact place where sea touches land, the damp strand of marvelous tracings.

The same land that was the land of the landing as Mox would say, that misty look in his eyes as he gazed out to sea. Dream cloth? Even I, a child, asked that. Where, down to earth, was the dock to hitch up the boat? Or even a big rock like the Pilgrims had? How could one say, then, that his special people, that historic band of gypsies, the very first gypsies to set bare foot on the soil of the new world, had been put ashore at this exact spot on the outer banks so long ago? Bodily deported from Scotland to North Carolina in 1710, wouldn't they more likely have been cast off at some regular port? Rim, Sinti or Manches? More like Celt Tinker Mox admitted, in fact proclaimed, progeny of earlier roving forebears who Painted Their Bodies Blue. Prodigious mysterious rock movers with a soft technology so smooth and elegant that it suspended gravity and rolled on air? So clever with the secret of vanishing that if necessary they could take sanctuary within the nodding petal cup of any handy cooperating wildflower?

What I was heir to! A magic small one among the abandoned on one side and the devalued deported on the other with the (now lost?) secret of how to move the world off its fulcrum with ease.

Now almost a dozen years later why couldn't I lay down the parting? Put it to sleep?

Wherever they were, Mox and Tranquilli, could they see me now and know that I had come to the age, the charmed age, to choose my own name?

"You have a name in you that's your real name," my father used to say, "everyone does."

Now again at the summit of our people-made mountain with the yang feed for the birds, I was sure. Then shivered. How can you cast off one self and be another? It's easy. If your new self is already there.

Hard too. I must be gentle with Mini, the small one, as I let her go. From a warm shelter within my own breathing I remembered her dimpled hands, her stubby little fingers, her plump pink palms. From the outside, externally, objectively, I looked down at my own hands, growing slender, supple, saying different things when they pointed or waved or stroked the tender air in a tender Stork Cools Wings; not one cell was the same, not one drop of blood, not one strand of now deeper burnished hair. Why, then, was it not easy to cast her off as a child dismissed at bedtime before an epic new day? Sleep, at least do me the favor of sleeping, Mini, I demanded. But even that was futile. If I was I was I yet she, the whole I of her was still within me flowing, growing, persisting in some enduring way that both affected and transcended physical change: Mini, mini, *mini*— Yes she was still there, familiar as morning noon and night, refusing to be put down even as she was outgrown, still asking all those questions, some smart, some dumb.

"I'm Mavis," I challenged her, then felt dashed. Mavis. Celtic for wood thrush. So okay. No one can sing like a wood thrush sings *but why can't I dance like a wood thrush sings?*

It was true. My claim if not to new naming then to something of essence yet unnamed lay deeper than any attempt to express it could show, its assurance secure within a forest dell that was, in turn, but a dim portal to deeper knowing. I shivered again. I remembered the haunting within the hush of forest dusk, the recurring mystery, the reliable miracle. It had left an indelible imprint, that preternatural call, its source unseen as spirit is unseen. Was it not as if the forest itself had been given voice in sudden fleeting release? Like spilled quicksilver transmitted into quicksilver sound it had been suddenly everywhere out of nowhere, making creation itself reverberate, reiterating again at dawn from realms within realms. I knew now part of the secret. Only in the deepest sanctuary of the forest and then only at dusk and dawn when earth is poised on a turning edge between light and dark can one hear the rare transcending cry of a mavis. It was she, Mini, the small one, absorbing, entranced, who had been there from the inside, marked for life by the ecstasy that no child can express, a part as the mute leaves were a part.

Yes I remembered, half dreaming like a bedded fawn with ears tuned to the ethereal. They said the source was a little bird, one you'd hardly notice, one seldom if ever seen, a secret nester.

Why couldn't I lay to rest what cried out for rest?

Way back then in that same forest, our secret place where All Things Come Together, I remember how my father changed his name. He was angry and kicked a giant pine tree. The force of the kick slammed back into his foot and ankle and, gasping, he came away limping. The tree was not hurt. It just stood there. Then Pax, still Pax then, came at a little sappling, a tender shoot, to bend it to cracking, to split, to uproot. But I jumped in front of the little tree and cried out and I stood there rooted like the tree itself, shaking. Pax laughed and said, "You're right, Titmouse," and he veered away into a handspring, favoring his injured foot. He limped, then, to a sunny spot where he lay down with his body in the shade and his bruised foot out in the sun. Kicking his boot off, he rotated the stunned ankle and wriggled his toes within nature's great spotlight, exposing the pad of his foot to the hot solar rays. "Aeich! That's good," he said, "y'know Mini it comes to me that Pax is not my real name. We wouldn't deceive 'em, would we?"

"Max," I reminded him, "you can't go back to Max."

"I outgrew it," he said, "it was getting too big for me."

"Pax?" I tried again, "couldn't you turn peaceful? What other name can you get to go with Tranquilli?" I was thinking of how they had tried for bond meaning and how it had to sound to the ear. "Tranquilli," he said, "another case of forced draft. As tranquil actually as— the center of a tropical storm?"

"Mox," I said his name out of the blue.

For a moment he looked startled. "Born but not shorn," he tried it on, "Mox with lox (locks)."

64

"You mean you had your big hair when you were a baby?" I tried to imagine a newborn with that huge mahogany mop.

"Mox," I stuck him the way a child sticks people with the truth, "You've always been Mox?"

Softly he began to chant a nonsense chant:

> "Mox, Mox
> strong as a fox
> shrewd as an ox
> Mox, Mox
> Interim Mox—"

"Interim," I asked, "what's that?"

"It's obvious. If you don't know, make up something to fit the case."

He drifted off to sleep, then, hands back of his head, looking like someone who had just swallowed something dubious and was trying to digest it in a dream.

* * *

Was I remembering all this as a borderline adult remembers, thinking child events but breathing into them mature meanings? There is this fiction that children are less aware, less keen or whole of feeling, a fiction I had vowed to never let stand, still crying out of my own beginnings. For I knew, looking both forward and back on a border of being, that a child feels as deeply as an adult, sometimes with a penetrating insight that becomes opaque in adults. The difference is that no words are there, or not enough words, or not the right ones to express as a grasp

65

on reality. But now I had words. Now I could put it together, that last time when we were still all there, that vivid but lost last time when we were innocently on the verge of parting. Now I could say what had never yet been said but what some time, somewhere, somehow, had to be said with words. As a kind of retroactive balm?

Yes it was that last time, a free time, our private holiday I thought, with food in the bags and the sky high and wide. We were back at the open ocean at that same place that is now Tranquilli's forever, on our gypsy outer banks at surf's edge where sands still blow free and limitless in the seashore preserve. We had gathered driftwood for a fire but no one had made a move to get the food out. I thought I knew what was up even before Mox took me to the water's edge and pointed back up North toward the wide misty swing of Hatteras. Up the beach there he told me, stooping down to my size and putting an arm over my shoulder, far up there around that first little bend, hidden from here, was a surprise. A secret till now. *Something never seen before.* "Take your treasure pail," he said, "and find it, who knows what? The stranger it is the better. But don't hurry. Take your time. In fact don't come back 'till the juniper's shadow is under the juniper like a skirt on the sand. Or when you stand tall and find you have no shadow at all."

I took the pail he held out because this was a do-it thing, not a question of this or that and, pouting, I started the trudge. I knew what was up. They were going to shut me out, the two of them. They were going to play their private game, Mox and Tranquilli. When it came to the

66

place where everything zeroes down to center, there were two of them, not three. So? It was all right to give me birth and say I belonged, I was one of them. Big deal. What good was a door when it was shut in your face?

"Your day will come, Mini," my father once said in a burst, "Don't worry. You too will know love all the way. You too will have a lover. Don't be afraid."

O! What was this thing as strong as anger yet not anger, as intense as pain yet a balm? A balm embracing and penetrating all in one, some kind of lightning whose stroke was tingling joy, a cry of bodies alive in each other.

Love in the extreme, love focused and blind to all else? Even to other loves?

SEVEN

LITTLE BROTHER

Smarting, rejected, shut out of the garden's innermost secret, I ran the last way to the juniper's shade around the bend, only vaguely looking for treasure. It was then that I saw him coming from the opposite direction farther up the beach, running, stopping now and then to fling a stone into the surf, a boy about my own age, a lone figure running toward where I was half hidden under the juniper spread. I sat still, a mouse under a leaf, waiting to see what he would do. As he came closer I saw he was a thin boy with a thin sober face, his hair clipped short like a flat patch of oat stubble atop his head. For a second I thought I was going to be overrun as he blindly headed for the farther side of the same sheltering bush in a kind of frantic rush; he was already sobbing when he hit the sand, his cries bursting out as if he could hold them in no longer. His sobs seemed to come with a squealing edge, wrenching, as abandoned as an infant's. I sat frozen in consternation. Although I had an impulse to reach out a hand to touch him I understood clearly, child that I was, that I was an intruder hearing what was

71

not meant for anyone else to hear. Under cover of his distress—he seemed to be trying to burrow under into the sand—I inched away noiselessly from my side of the low hanging shaggy shrub until finally I rolled over the brink of a small sand bank, toppling down the face of it, safely hidden from view. His sobs could still be heard but muffled now, leveling off, sporadic.

It was snug in the wind-sculpted little valley in the sand hillock and I felt distant from the troubled boy as I sat hugging my knees beneath a sheltering crest of sea oats. I looked out over the water hoping for dolphins. Dolphins, if possible, close to shore, close enough to talk to, pat, maybe ride along on a flipper, *hug*. What was so unreasonable about that? Next I leapt up and raced for the shore, turning cartwheels at every few steps. I had forgotten about the boy and was still peering out and scanning the waves when I felt a pelting shock of sand spattered over my back, spurting up even into my hair in a gritty shower. Elbow up to shield my eyes I turned to see him standing a few feet behind me, grinning, both hands wadded full for a second blast.

"Hold it," I shouted into the wind, "I'm watching for dolphins—"

He hardly looked like the same boy, keen and sharp now, no way forlorn. Although his eyelids were red and puffy, his eyes were dry. "Dolphins," he retorted, "you're crazy. There's no dolphins here. Sharks mabe. But no dolphins."

"Why not? It's an ocean. They can go anywhere—"

"Not here," he was positive, "I never seen dolphins here. If I never saw—"

"Just because you never saw—" I stuck with it, then drew back; a second stinging blast hit me, this one across the stomach and down all across my legs. With my arms crossed to shield my body I turned on him, "Why did you do that?"

"Because you got no clothes on," he accused.

I looked down. So? It was summer. Warm. This was our free place. No one around but our own. "You're almost all bare yourself," I defended myself, pointing to his brief bathing trunks, "take the rest off and see how good it feels—"

"My old man would kill me," he countered, "I'd get belted to hell." His voice carried a burden of threat.

"He's not here," I pointed out, "what about your mother?" I was trying to latch onto any answer he'd accept but this suggestion only brought more scorn, "She don't count," he said, "she's got nothing to say."

I turned some handsprings to show what I could do but he wasn't watching; he had run back to wet against a high bank and it was then, with his back turned, that I first noticed the welts across his shoulders and ribs, angry red stripes that could be seen even at that distance. When he turned around to come back he was still stuffing his tender little peenie into his trunks and he saw me watching. I decided not to say anything about the welts because, like the sobbing, they seemed a secretly exposed unmentionable thing. He was grinning again as he ran

73

back straight to me, "Where's your manny," he accused, "you got nothing—you know—" Now he pointed to me all smooth down front.

Could it be that this pushy little brother, besides being sore and smarting, didn't know the difference between girls and boys? I thought he was teasing and I ran to the shore and plopped a stone into the surf. He followed close behind and when he saw me toss the stone he stooped to select a flat smooth pebble and then with a skillful underhand twist he sent it zinging and skimming over the surface of the water in a straight line through one, two, crests before it bounded and rebounded on a glassy trough and sank. I couldn't help but clap. It was beautiful. Could we be friends after all? I had never gotten the hang of skipping stones but something stopped me from asking for help. "You couldn't do it in a million years," he was saying. I swung, then, into some figures, imagining a balance bar at the tide line. I did the best I could muster and then in a final flourish stepped up to a Seven Star Pose. He was staring straight at me but he made no move to applaud. "Do you want me to show you how?" I asked. "Why should I learn that stuff from you," he was quick to answer, "when I can do better before I even try?"

One thing was sure. This boy couldn't be Andy. No way. No way at all. For one thing his name was Belittle, that was clear. No way could he be the twin brother I was always looking for as my own special partner for the act, the Andy to my Anne.

"Girls are freaks," he confided as if he expected automatic agreement, "you haven't got nothing—you know—" Once more he made that gesture down front.

Now the anger I had been swallowing burst out; I knew the answer to that one because Tranquilli had told me, the fantastic, the beautiful answer, "I've got plenty!" I shrieked, "but it's all inside!"

Tell him about the tender flower with the hidden stem leading back into the secret chamber where new life itself could start? Never. The mother cell and the father cell joining like in love to form the tender new one who would start smaller, even, than a pea in a pod? Never. Not in a million years. "Show me," he was demanding, "if you've got so much, show me—"

For one moment the boy looked around as if to make sure we were still alone on the beach, then he came at me with arms flailing; with a flash he jumped in front of me with his hands beating the air all around yet not quite touching, "If you don't show me," he threatened, "I'll throw you down and stuff your mouth full of sand."

I too looked around; in a lurid flash I saw that the juniper shade was like a skirt on the sand and where I stood I had no shadow at all. Mox! Tranquilli! "Never," I screamed, "not in a million years!" I turned this way and that but he was always there blocking ahead of me and now he was making faces to boot—supposed to be funny as well as scary?— a series of twisted masks, tongue out and wagging, eyes popping, mouth screwed to a tooth-barred grin. "Not funny," I made a scary face too in self-defense and once more I tried to escape from the flailing circle as he burst into a taunting singsong chant.

In the end instinct and timing came to my rescue. As

he lunged to grab me I stood there a fractured second as if rooted, not retreating, but just before his fingers could close on an arm I found myself doing a flash Repulse Monkey on an oblique line to the rear off to the left. Before he could recover from his surprise I followed with another Repulse Monkey off to the right. As my trailing hand came around I barely brushed his shoulder and upper arm, a shadow touch with only a shadow of push, yet he pitched forward with the force of his own thrust and went sprawling face down on the sand.

Now I knew I was in trouble. Could I outrun him? I started racing down the beach, then, toward the bend, toward home camp. But I was brought up short by a sight ahead. Just then, trying to flee, was when I saw it, an animal hump on the sand just above the high water mark, some creature, not moving. A beached dolphin?

I stopped and turned around to shout and beckon, forgetting all fear of the boy. It was almost comical to see him still lying there flat on his stomach, head raised like a turtle testing the air to venture out of its shell after an affront, his hands spread to hoist his weight. At that distance I could feel the gaze of his bright amber eyes boring into me as if he were seeing me for the first time. "Come on," I shouted, waving him on, "a beached dolphin!"

As I came even with the creature I did not need the boy to tell me it was not a dolphin and that it was dead, but that's what he did tell me as soon as he came up, "It's a shark," he shouted, "can't you tell the difference between a dolphin and a stinking shark?"

It was true. It was a baby shark, no longer than I was tall, perfect in every detail from upright tail fin and side gills to flattened round toothy snout. Or mabe it was only a grown dogfish, who could tell the difference? But whether an infant or a grown miniature, in either case dead. There wasn't a mark on it but its little pig eyes had already started to turn to gelatin and were weeping down the sides of its jaw. I remember feeling a surge of pity for the strange gap-mouthed forlorn inert "little" thing, at the same time being thrilled to be so close to the un-touchable breed, supposedly deadly even when young. How had it died without a mark showing? Why did it still seem almost alive, dead-eyed but somehow still knowing? Above all, and this was the pitiful part, why with its fierceness all gone did it seem doubly exposed and helpless? Like everyone else if it had to eat it had to eat because—it had to eat? I put a toe out and felt cau-tiously along the smooth-looking but tough hide of the side nearest me—

"Stand back," shouted Foss—that's what his name turned out to be, Foss for Foster—"Stand back and I'll kill it."

He had armed himself with a piece of driftwood, a fragment of decking out of some old wreck that still had a rusty bolt embedded in one end, and he started to hack at the sharklet's tail. Raising the weapon over his head he brought it down with a sharp thwack, hard, punctur-ing the skin with a fizzing sound; an almost colorless fluid spewed out and a stench along with it. In a frenzy as if not satisfied with the result he next raked the metal tip along the flesh of the side I had touched, trying to tear open its vitals. "The guts," he screamed, "let's spill its guts—"

"It's already dead," I protested, "why are you killing it all over again?"

"Because it's bad," once more his voice was full of scorn, "don't you even know that?"

Thwarted in ripping open the torso, next the boy, still in a frenzy, aimed a bare foot at the tooth-filled gaping mouth of the young shark-spawn; only to lurch away howling. Human blood. His big toe was dripping, the ball of his foot flowing red as if after a razor slash.

I felt his shock, creature empathy spontaneous.

"The crud, get the crud off."

Young as I was I knew what to do; if you step on a cutting shell, Mini, if you ever step on a cutting shell. "The crud," I insisted, "get in the water and wash off the crud."

Then I remembered there was more. If it flows blood press it with cloth, clean if you can make it but in any case *press it*. "Press it," I screamed in frustration at his blocked response, "take your pants off! Press it!"

But he had no ears for me even though for one moment, hesitating, he looked back with a long locked look. Then he was limping away, heeling it back toward the place he had come from, back toward the only ones he could trust. "They'll kill me," he sobbed, his voice again taking on that squealing edge, trying to skip-limp, favoring his bleeding foot as he limp-raced or tried to race.

I stood watching him until he disappeared around the bend farther up the beach.

He was gone.

I turned and looked down at the dead shark. Three of its teeth appeared to sag slightly and they were bloodied. On impulse I picked up a handful of sand and drizzled it over the bloody teeth for some kind of cover, hearing some of the loose grains trickle down into the dried dead maw, "That's for the boy you hurt," I told the beast.

EIGHT

IN THE GARDEN

As I turned the point and ran for home camp I could see the two of them far down the beach, little figures moving around a fire, Tranquilli in the flimsy white burnoose-like thing she wore at the shore to protect her vulnerable skin, Mox with a beach towel draped around his middle like an Indian dhoti, his bare back even at that distance gleaming a sunscorched brown. Eating! How unfair could they get? As I came close I stamped my feet, I screeched, I spit on the sand. They turned then and saw me and both laughed. "Come," said Tranquilli, "eat. We saved some for you." She handed me a chunk of pan bread sopped in the broth of the dish du jour and in spite of a lingering smart I gulped it down.

When I had eaten my fill I went back toward a sheltering dune and lay down and made an angel in the pure rippled sand, the kind winter kids make in new snow. Mox came and sat at arms length and he touched one finger to my finger where my reach was stretched out like a wing, "You've just been created," he announced, "sit up and say what it's like."

"You mean I've just been born? I've just popped out of my mother's womb?"

"Even more. It's the first day of creation and you're the first one to breathe and see—"

"You mean you're God painted on the ceiling and I'm the first—man?"

We sometimes acted out pictures and none of this was unusual.

"The first human, Titmouse, human. In your case mere human."

"You lie!" I spat. Why should my smouldering grievance be rolled over with some of his sleight of hand? He had not even noticed that I had not brought back my treasure pail, much less returned with something truly magical to show. Clearly he did not care about any of that, the pail abandoned under the juniper spread far up the beach, forsaken, gone, lost. As for treasure—

"But Titmouse of course you can be the first one. Aren't you just as—hum-m—*representative* of what's human as—say—some big muscled gracefully sprawled male athlete or—ah—yes by God old Adam himself, created as a fresh born squalling babe out of womon but cosmically refusing to this day to admit it—" He was still sailing on his own tack, now apparently oblivious to me the new first one.

"Shark's teeth. Bloody," I almost sobbed, "you lied."

"I've got it," he only seemed to answer. His eyes had that sweeping far away look, his face glowing as it did whenever he glimpsed a new turn in an old play. For the act, that's what he was thinking, could it be adapted for

84

the act? "We'll repaint the mural on the caravan," he declared, "God in evidence only as a beam of light touching you dear one, touching you. Yes you Titmouse." Now he was looking at me almost as if seeing me, "You are there, the real one, no myth, a created fact in flesh and blood, a wee orange-haired womonchild with a sassy face and womb intact, no mere afterthought rib for eternal cosmic ribbing. Titmouse on the Sistine. That'll shake 'em up—"

Was it useless to try to get his attention? I looked down toward surf's edge and saw Tranquilli there, her light garment hoisted up and billowing around her thighs as she stepped gingerly over shell fragments and pebbles, cooling her feet in the trashing foam. Should I race down and ram my head into what she herself called the crying place, that soft spot under her breasts on her abdomen at just my height where I could fling myself as necessary, face buried, sobs muffled, assured of the solace of her encircling arms no matter what. But something Mox had said had caught my fancy after all: to come alive full blown and aware, seeing detail sharp and whole as if for the first time. I sat up then and stared around. I felt the hard sand under the plump of my butt, cool now with the damp below the hot dry surface granules. I was sitting on earth and it was the whole earth I was sitting on like on top of a huge ball, that much I understood. Straight through who was sitting on the other side? What would be at the other end of a plumb line from the exact spot on the outer banks at the edge of the ocean where I was pressing a human seat mark in the sand? Running, standing, *swimming,* could my twin brother be there at that other pole, was that the only place I could find him? Actually of course even I didn't believe anything as sheer madeup as that. Out of dream cloth they would say.

Loose sand was sifting through the sparse sea oats in the hot wind and I felt stinging prickles all along my spine and over my back and arms and legs. But it was gentle and vagrant, each prickling grain but a tingling reminder of feeling, of being alive. I licked my lips and tasted gritty salt. I smelled the ocean, the great thrumming endless water down there thrashing in and sucking out in a glassy race beneath the next spume mountain spill, the breakers cresting and crashing, the rollers soughing and gurgling high on the strand. The smell of earth-sea in love, in the raw. Suddenly I felt my lungs gulping air, filling a great gasping gulf. Without being conscious of it I had been holding my breath while I felt and saw and listened. Now my lungs, alive on their own, gulped air like a swimmer breaking surface.

Mox was still talking. What was he saying? Did it matter? He had moved to the crest of the nearest dune face, peering out to sea. "You lied to me," I still complained but gently now; after all he had moved beyond hearing. "There was no treasure—"

"There is always treasure," he was shouting from the top of the bluff, "always! How could I lie about a thing like that? *Always* something never seen before—"

Was he reading my mind or merely catching up with what I had said earlier? I lay back again, then, and studied the sky, a world-hovering wingsing diaphanous up-sidedown bowl with clouds floating free, mountains of luminous white showing vast caverns and ravines from the down side up. Some lower level wisps raced in what seemed an almost touchable layer but constantly chang-ing, elongating, evaporating to form again who knows where. Then as if in response to my inner reach all the clouds seemed to part at once on an immense arch of pure vaulting blue and a single gull came and hung in the center above me, testing the currents and hanging there for a magic moment like a translucent kite, his body in balance, his smooth head moving from side to side on a level plane as if to survey the scene. Sun so bright it hurt the eyes streamed through his semi-opaque glowing body, his bone structure outlined almost as in an x-ray, the wing bones gracefully reaching out from shoulder to tip like arms ending in pinions instead of fingers. His feet, almost crossed but not quite, lay neatly retracted under his tail. Then he dove. Off a brink of air into azure space. Gliding down, sailing up again in a wide arc with hardly a movement of his outstretched wings. Now he was coming round again, positioning—eee-ee!—off again. In fact again and again. For pleasure, for play, what else? Obviously he was not spying or rousting for food, a dead crab on the beach, a flashing fin just under the surface of a wave, the melon rinds we had thrown out for his tribe to scavenge. No it had to be for sheer joy, riding some stream of air as it plunged over an in-visible falls in the sky. I jumped up at the exact moment

87

when Mox shouted from the bank above and Tranquilli waved from the beach below, pointing out to sea. What was up?

Mox was down off the bluff in a flash and near me pitched forward half prone on the sand, one knee flexed forward in brace position, the other leg extended to the rear at a slant. I needed no further invitation; it was the cue to mount to our shoulder stand. I flung myself at his back in a flying leap, parallel on a slant as he rose, our hands clasped at the sides to augment balance telescoped within momentum, I upright on his shoulders at the pulse-timed instant that he stood full, my height true and straight above his height.

Dolphins!

A whole pod!

Little whales, our friends in the sea.

From atop my top place I saw a ruffling of the surface of the water in the middle distance like waves within waves, exploding and leaping, waves scattering waves, arching, the circle sign over and over, bodies sleek and in unison yet alternating, a rondelet timed and in tune yet madly spontaneous it seemed. Chattering too. They were talking and calling among themselves. In *delphanese*. Or *porpocine* as some call it. I screamed as Mox swung me to the ground and we dashed to the edge of the water world, splashing in, calling, shouting. The froth of a breaker hit me in the face as if in wild greeting, I raised up, let it take me. Mox was chest deep in a trough with his hands up to crest the crest. There is this old saying, y'know, where dolphins run never fear sharks.

But the impact and swirling tow of the water was burying me and I struggled dripping back to the solid strand as the best place to see, to call, to fly with leaps and to wave. What I was trying to do of course was to invite them in to shore. What then? Let come what would. Can one imagine the details of magic before magic happens? But of one thing be sure. This was not something made up out of dream cloth. This was brighter than a dream and it was squealing real.

"Don't scare 'em," Tranquilli was cautioning from her spot at surf's edge, "Gentle—gently—sing a flute song—" She had taken off her head scarf and was letting it stream out full in the wind stream, tweaking the anchored end of the cloth in her hand just enough on a rhythmic beat so that the long white filmy banner seemed to undulate in the air in time with the dolphins' communal ballet. Let's hope they see it, I thought, and know they have nothing to fear *because to clear the ground of fear is to clear the ground for you dear*. Who said that? I couldn't remember but the rhymed phrase had popped into my head ready-made, full blown.

Now, incredibly, the dolphins seemed to be coming closer, the profiles of individual bodies visible as they leaped within the sparkling medley, their communicating clicks and piping whistles and human-sounding squeals more distinct to the ear. In a rather tight arc, a detectable turn, they were swinging from the east out of the deeps of the ocean into what appeared to be a shallower course parallel to the shore on a line due south. True they were not close enough to touch. Nothing like that. But I had a feeling, as certain as the feel of the firm gritty sand under my feet, that they could see us even as we could see them. Then the incredible itself exploded. As the trailing end of the formation swung around so that some seemed to be milling around in place while others had to race to catch up along the fringes, several individuals began to fantail, that is to stand upright out of the water with tails slapping the surface before they arched forward in a series of elegant water-slicing nosedives. I saw that those at the far edges of this turning fringe were positioned closest to land and I had already run to the water to be closer from our side, standing knee deep in foam but with feet braced against the sucking undertow. It was just then at that closest point that a young one, no longer than I was tall, suddenly leaped up and fantailed like a sassy precocious brat, his "bottle nosed" mouth wide open and pouring out a highpitched wordlike torrent in my direction, eyeing me even as I eyed him; for one startling moment our seeing locked, joined, lucid as light caught in the crystalline lens of some deeper inner eye, creaturely cognition bonded in an illumined exchange.

The leap of a knowing spark from out of the water world and an affirming throb from the realm of land?

Undulating as he slapped the surface to stay upright, suddenly the little dolphin was gone as he pitched forward with a slight sidewise movement, going under broadside with what may have been an unskilled thwack. From my side, limp, trembling but still jumping and also crying out as he had done, I waited for him to surface again. I was not unrewarded. Farther out and away he leaped up again, briefly fantailed, then was gone.

"Don't get lost," I called out with a sudden twinge of concern for his safety, "don't get left behind," I realized that he could not linger to play, that he had to stay with his people to survive.

"Go! Go! Don't get left behind—"

NINE

DIP FOR TREASURE

BENEATH THE SEA

I looked around then. Near me I saw that Tranquilli was standing motionless, her scarf limp in her hand. She opened her arms and I flew to—the crying place? No—the squealing place. No weeps. I almost pushed her over in the rush and she staggered backward, recovering then as she clutched me for support in a swaying mutual hug.

In a series of brush steps I went up the beach. I did an Iron Back Hand with thrust and swagger and then I Carried The Tiger To The Mountain, staggering like a bulging world, pregnant, exaggerated and raffish, imagining a pliant pussy cat curled up in swollen arms, tiger-sized of course, poured out of nothing into something purring the color of stripes and sun gold. My pace was irregular, too fast, and when I came to the Repulse Monkey I thrust out, uncentered, unsmooth, racing senselessly and I didn't care. I floated, I blended with the breeze then reined it in as if trying to put the wind itself into a cornered pattern. It couldn't be done. There was no use contending with the wind. I struck out, broke silence with a shout, then gave it up. I had come to Dip

For Treasure Beneath The Sea and for a moment stood gasping, puffing, gulping every breath as a joyous exchange.

I looked back at Tranquilli and remembered that Dip was the one figure she could not do because it involved stooping, a whole wide scoop as deep as the sea; for this one she always paused in rest position as if hanging for support on her own arms and the air. Out of some depth of familiarity with all the salubrious elements when she paused a beat she yet never missed a beat. It was a skill I had yet to become one with, the real pace, the pace of being, never hurrying but never ceasing. In time, that is, with time itself? Out of my own unending flow of time I took her all in as an unharsh lesson, reliably there, as durable as day and night.

I saw that she was staring at something in the water at her feet, pointing, making little gestures as if to stoop.

"Don't stoop—don't stoop—" I ran back to her, "Don't stoop!"

She was pointing to a small stone, nothing much more than a pebble, one among piles and myriads. It didn't seem unusual to me but she insisted, singling it out with her toe. I brought it up dripping, offering it like a jewel on my palm. It was glistening wet but already fading dull dry as she took it in her hand and turned it over, studying it with absorption. "It runs clear through," she marvelled. She spit on it, then, to bring out the sheen brighter than polish, "Seaweed. Petrified seaweed. Caught in the stone. Alive. Who knows. A million years—"

I pondered carefully before answering, "A million million at least," I confirmed soberly; million was just a word, a familiar term meaning yes, sure, you're right. Or when you looked up at the night sky and saw a million as million is; the uncountable, *there*, in focus, beyond understanding, an arching sparkling fact, too much, goodby, never mind. "—the night sky is a mirror of all that is in the sea not seen in day, upside down, some kind of—" Where had I heard that? Or had I heard it? Dream cloth?

But Tranquilli was not listening, still absorbed in the stone. I took it from her, spit on it routinely to recapture the sheen, saw the green streak sliced in it as well as across it, stone as stone, lacery, tracery.

"Parsley for Posterity?" she asked, beaming.

It was a private joke, insubstantial, from nowhere. Mox had once called something similar sea parsley and we had, spontaneously, senselessly, collapsed in a shower of giggles. Rib-tingling. As stressful as crying but delicious. For no reason. Except that the sun, maybe, was tickling our toes through the flickering ripples of the shallow shore wavelets?

"Even the stones, Mini, even the stones—" Tranquilli's voice now was sober but in a light arching way.

"Alive?"

"When they go to the stars, Mini, the stones—"

As I handed the little stone back to her it suddenly occurred to me, my mother's real name. Of course I had known it all along. I had just never dared give it voice. But now it was so apparent it seemed it had to be recognized in words. It was in the light refracted off the dancing prancing water, diffused, everywhere, yet particular in fingering beams reflected not only on her but from her. The effect was heightened by the exposed brightness of her billowing garment and that of her pale skin that seemed to have a pearl tone luminosity now, *not* blue but suggesting a delicate tint below the surface. Yes, her characteristically pale complexion that would never "take the sun" as we said, as always dramatically accented by her dark eyes and long straight black hair. The point is the light was there over all, too much, the real thing had to be said. Yet I felt an unexpected timidity, for some unaccountable reason suddenly shy. "Light-of-the-Sea—" I tried out the words cautiously.

She looked up, only half smiling. She appeared, in fact, perplexed as if trying to make out words that were hard to hear or confused in meaning. Surely she could not be displeased?

The surf flooded in with a long singing sigh and rippled out close to silence, an interlude between the thrashing of the big ones. "What did you say?" Her voice was close to herself.

Now it was my turn to listen to what was not quite clear.

"Light-of-the-Sea," I repeated, trying to be more firm, daring in myself but smiling a little guiltily, I did not know why, "your real name."

She did not answer. The laughing gulls with their neat 'screwed on' dark heads were screeching and circling over the spot near where we had eaten, a sudden noisy bit. A huge roller piled up on the beach and collapsed just short of where we stood; Tranquilli moved back a step or two but I held my position, taking the splash up to my thighs, "You know, like at twilight," I digressed to what seemed safer ground, "the light in the sea shining out of the water in the dark—"

I had changed the image as if retreating but the new one did not seem inappropriate either. I was thinking next of the sparkling luminescence that blanketed the whole coast at unpredictable and rare intervals. I did not know that the strange shifting glow, so bright it could sometimes light up low lying night clouds, was caused by uncountable minute phosphorescent lifeforms. The phenomenon was simply our glory night, a mystery to me but no more a mystery than almost everything. One thing about such luminosity, of course, it proved for me beyond a doubt that our earth was not a dark star, that old Hera could glow on her own if she tried. In turn that meant that in the realm of All That Is she was less likely to ever become lost or go astray from those who loved her. Had not Tranquilli herself told me of one rescue in an extremity, of how the poor fainting dove, released upon the face of a world flood from the only boat afloat, had been heartened in her brave endeavor to find hope for the humans and animals? And by this very thing, the light-of-the-sea suddenly glowing from horizon to horizon, illuminating in stark but merciful outline the emerging tiny islet, at first just big enough for the soles of the dove's feet on a twig of a tender new olive tree. *Was she going to go back on me now?* Tranquilli, that is.

I detected a pensiveness, even a sadness, in her unexpected hesitance. I who named everything, everyone, would she be rejecting me in some nameless way if she rejected my bright name for her? What was wrong? With a feeling of wavering shame it suddenly came home to me that my naming must be in words weighted with more than a literal meaning. She had sometimes seemed to chafe at being called Tranquilli; yet was it not her own choice, her cover that she dare not leave on pain of—? O! Stripped of defense by my own blunder I felt (what I thought was) her pain and consternation. A wayward vision stabed into my mind. That place smelling of drugs and fear, that horrible day last year, that clinic we had blundered into in desperation, that intern before we fled saying to Mox within earshot of a gasping Tranquilli, "Amazing. A case for the journals. Tell me, how had a blue baby been able to live so long?"

In my eager thoughtlessness was I as—as—*cruel*— as that fledgling medicine man? *Blue tints?* I was dashed. It was as if to blot out all that with strong light she had taken on the glow of the sun and it was too painful to look in her direction. But no. I was wrong. Mercy was my friend. She was smiling now, that reined-in smile, but smiling now. Her voice sounded as if it came from a distance.

"Luz," she said, "luz marina."

Was she trying on the name after all, toned down with no sharp cadences in the liquid tones of the language she had come to claim as native by default?

But she was shaking her head, softly rejecting yes, but also marvelling. She drew me to her as if I would need comfort (or she didn't want me to see her face?), I once more secure in that warm breathing place from which all solace flowed. Above me, all around me, her voice sounded cheerful. "Beautiful," she declared, once more open and sharing, "but taken, Mini, taken—you know— Besides, don't worry—"

Why should I worry if she was not hurt and I was still in favor? Was it not the name that had come to me as though it had some illumined if hidden meaning? But she continued to hold me against her as if there were more to be said that wouldn't bear the light of face-to-face awareness; with my ear close to her breathing and a whisper from her heart I felt her breath catch, heard her blood murmur in that catch and—I held my own breath—pulse, thank mercy, even, regular, like everyone's. The interior world, mysterious and frightening and wonderful. With a happy bonus signal. The sprightly but mundane gurgling of her stomach was comforting enough for a small belly laugh. "Don't worry," I reassured her.

"Don't worry," she repeated, "You know. There's something I should remind you of."

Her voice had that special tone. What was coming? Was she going to tell me again about my day, the first one, my birth day? That time, how had she said it and I had overheard, "I was not brave. I was not crazy. But I was determined. Against all advice and Mox's—*entreaty*—yes, even against *the blue thing* itself I said I will have this child. To show a small one—okay?—what it is not to be abandoned."

Or maybe she would say deserted. Somehow it sounded less dreadful.

I tensed against her but, relax, this time she was only saying something about the sun and the sea and the land and "all that flows through them. That, Mini, that knowing that—waiting for you, like—" She paused short of breath, then flowed on as if to meet something that had to be surmounted, "If it should ever come to that, if I should ever have to leave, remember—"

Precipitously I clamped my hands over my ears to blot out her next words. "Leave." *Tight.* Still held against her body I blocked my hearing as if life depended on it. My face, I knew, was twisted in a grimace against her abdomen; if she ever had to—*leave?*

When I finally took my hands away from my ears all that was left to hear was the frayed end, "—with luz marina. You will take Mox by the hand and you will lead him to the mountain."

I looked up seeking her face. She was smiling and I smiled back.

I hugged her and freed myself.

All was well again? *Real?* No more words?

I waited for her to say more, fair is fair. But no, she appeared content again, through with talking. She handed me the little stone and I felt its smooth satiny surface like a reassurance. I held it in my hand for a moment then put it on top of my head in a tangle of hair because I was still bare of clothes and had no pockets. I walked

102

down the beach, then, away from Tranquilli, looking for more treasures.

* * *

The wind had dropped. The shadows stretched longer from the dunes. The white light of high day was off the face of the sea and the oblique sun brought out more color in the water, deep seething blue in the troughs, grey-green where the caps still flung their spume. The detail of distant waves was clear and sharp in the lowering sunlight that seemed aimed, now, straight at them like a spotlight, glowing strong from the West, reflecting bright but thin from the East. Although cooling spread with the shadows, in the narrowing stretches of sunlight the golden air still snapped warm and sparkling.

I picked my way down the beach, never quite catching up with three sandpipers who seemed to be exploring the saltwater pools trapped in patches of seaweed cast up at tideline. The long strands of tangled rubbery tissue, glistening red-yellow with a tincture of green, had the tint and smell of iodine I thought, not delicate in texture like my sea parsley, but tough as rope turned slick, slippery. I squished my bare feet through it then drew back when I was caught by the stinging edge of something unseeable. A minute broken shell? Some tiny creature defending its domain? I could find no wound. But now I kept free of the threatening mat.

I almost stumbled over Mox. He was lying at shoreline all but supine, half in and half out of the water, propped back on his elbows with his upper arms bulging under the stress of his own relaxed weight. When he saw me coming he tipped his head back over his shoulders, maneuvering a mollusk's view of me and the arching sky above. His great mop of wiry midnight red hair (the color of polished mahogany we always said) spilled backward over the salty grit. It was his candid vanity, his unabashed joy, one of the really good things in life, but I had a giggling impulse to run my feet through the curly spread. Better than stinging seaweed! I almost made it but he anticipated my foray and in teasing defense snatched backward at my feet with one hand. I eluded his upsidedown reach as deftly, as counter cleverly as if I had singing bells on my ankles.

"Tomorrow it's back to hit the bit Mini," he called out.

His voice was on top of it all but his message wasn't. What he was saying was bread's low and when he called me Mini it meant business. I resented this intrusion of the nesessitous into our last hours of free time and I took a few lively grace steps farther beyond his reach. "I'm making up some new figures," I told him.

"People Pound Pavements," he offered.

"Loon Swallows Moon," I countered.

I was thinking of the silver TV moon we had seen in the department store window off the street that night, with the man doll figure in robot clothes prancing slowly as if dancing in liquid. Have you ever seen a loon up to his side-to-hind knees standing in still silver water in the full moonlight? Back on earth, that is. *In light too much to bear.*

104

I almost tripped over the discarded hulk of a horseshoe crab shell and then, in avoiding it, in turn almost stepped on a tiny live sand crab concealed in the shelter of the dark hump. The spidery little creature scurried sidewise out of my way, pausing at a safe distance to zap me with a baleful look from her stalk eyes.

TEN

SOMETHING

NEVER SEEN BEFORE

I was drawn with a sense of expectancy in the direction the dolphins had taken, South, down the beach the opposite way from where I had gone in the morning.

Time had yielded to timelessness and I moved down the tideline with the deliberate aimlessness of total spontaneity, attracted by a shard of sand-scoured greenglass here, a cluster of broken razor clam shells there, running to examine a sodden old shoe, half-burried, cast up flotsam from who knows where. Small, naked, unlost, I was infused with the realization that I was exactly where I wanted to be when I wanted to be there, at the edge of water and land between day and night, as if the here and the now had fused into one lucid sense of being. For the time *between* was almost upon us. When we would greet the coming of the *yin* as earth rose to douse the sun in parting splendor. The time to toe on universal center line, as we said, to regain perfect balance, to get in tune and so on. Well let them do it without me tonight, Mox and Tranquilli, in twosome, their shadows blending, parting, separate but in unison. To peer into the interstices between The Way Things Are and All That Is as Mox would say. Or simply to celebrate The Whole as Tranquilli would say. And me? What would I say? Nothing. To do it with body words was enough. I paused in my meandering drift southward to make a prefunctory but efficient Square Horse, conceding to the West and blending in self with the muted but glowing ember-red orb of the sun now skimming the crest of the dunes. Properly, anciently, I Covered My Weapon and bowed to the still arching but slightly subdued day and, in the same gesture, equally, to the yet hidden but coming night.

For one stilly moment the silence was as close as a friend.

Far down the beach, around another slight bend, how soon was it that I saw it? Something new. Something never seen before. Had Mox meant what he said afterall?

It was an aery ball, the size it's hard to say, large enough to fill the whole eye with startle, small enough to run to with arms outstretched to try to catch. A *live* beach ball? It was hanging—or was it touching?—just where the tide runs, the color of both sea and land.

I ran to look close and it receded out on the undertow, rising again above a rippling wave and slowly revolving in toward where I stood, not spun in water but floating above. Fragile cloud-like wisps enveloped its outer surface and under this shifting cover a sparkling spill of white, as of crystals, marked opposite poles. The fleeting impression of what lay under the vapor was blue and smooth, but all of this on closer glimpse (as it passed near and then again receded) turned out to be an illusion.

110

No. It was damp with more than vapor. Under the shifting cover it was girdled with crystal fluid along with patches of solids, some large, some small, some mere dots here and there as of a deeper underlayer breaking surface, mostly green but actually—now!—almost close enough to touch—of many colors. With ridges and cunning bumps and intricate tracings as well as large flat places, some bare, some lush and running with silver rivulets or pocked with irregular pools. Let it come close again! Let me see! Why was my heart warmed, making itself known?

Also what was that sound? It was like a ringing in the ears as of a million cicadas, muted but vibrant. Or of steam escaping in a dream, the voices of all time and of all creatures compressed in a steady state hiss and signaling—what? Did the sound, inaudible beyond me, come from inside me apart from the ball, some lingering swim water lodged in the inner ear?

I tipped to one side and shook the opposite foot, pounding my head.

Or was the whole thing far stranger? Was the sound, not as sound but as a silent signal coming from the ball, my auditory nerve amplified as a living receiver, a receptor receiving not only the unheard but the unhearable? I clapped my hands to both ears as the ball returned once again and the sound went on inside my head with neither increase or decrease. My hands could not shut out the deeper proof. The sound was not from inside me alone. The ball, silent, was emitting a message. What?

My heart knew. Once more the tight bloody muscle

111

that beat out the count of my life leaped, pulsing again, then, steady but stronger as with the beat of the sea.

Fragile beauty! Speak without words dear. Who will hear?

Now it was swinging back. It was coming again. Each time with a surprise, the never seen, never known, bright and visual, the veil not pierced but illumined, transparent. This time I must be ready with burning microscopic sight to see deep, deep. Now it appeared to be coming straight for me, closer than ever. Now! For one moment I seemed immersed in all that it was yet seeing distinct as from a clear distance. It was pulsing with life. Its fluid depths were teeming, its exposed parts were trembling, crawling, even its rooted tendrils were reaching, curling, responding.

But more. How could I say it? In its living entity it was of a different order from either some mythical cosmic handiwork, or yet from an object of life support whose secrets could be extracted only on demand from outside. In either case it would have to be approached from over and above rather than from within, earth split from heaven, the real from the ideal, nature from itself. Here the body of reality was revealed as just that, a body, inviolate in its relatedness among its parts. As I breathed it breathed in multiform dimensions, an organism as I was of it an organism. The heart and mind and touch and seeing of its own, then, could grow within the knowing that was already in them as part of it? The knowing out of Source within a whole? Lifesphere! Familiar mystery, the nature of the Nature of Being; in its *embodiment—*

112

I sat down limp on the wet sand, feeling a tingling along my spine. I grasped a handful of sand and scattered worlds within worlds upon the sea. A mist was closing in now as if saying something not by words but by enveloping. Inside the cooling embrace it was at once darkling and dazzling and now the ball, out there still, seemed to glow faintly even as it grew indistinct, swinging out and again lost in the rising fog. Was it twinkling or did I imagine it? Don't go. Never go. Never! This time no longer seeing it *I felt its presence near as a damp impress on the flat of one arm.* I saw, then, marvelling, that the skin over the pulse of my left wrist was wet. I stared before I rubbed some of the salty moisture on my cheek and then touched lips to wrist, a breeze on a breeze. I felt the earth beneath my body, the water lapping my feet with a touch more gentle, more subtle even than that of the most loving hand—

pearl, amber and coral of sea
jet, jade and multicrystal of land
clay, all
colors
quickened in flesh, fin,
wing, fur and fabulous
iris of eye

Again I tossed a handful of sand into the air hearing it dimple the glassy surface of the dark roller that was approaching as a moving wall of living fluid, fearsome as awe in leash. With a gracious gurgle it fanned out with

113

sensitive touch over the rocks, the pebbles, the shells at shore's edge.

From far up the beach I could hear them calling—

calling—

calling—

I did not want to answer. I could not lift a finger. I could not find my voice. Yet I knew that in time I must move, break the spell, for the tide had turned. It was coming in.

For the moment, timeless, true to scale but a part of scope, I lay back floating in space, hanging there, suspended, a part. The last wisps of fog had vanished and the familiar clear black dome of the universe came down all around, darkness a sparked setting for celestial lights, the breathing earthnight sprinkled and glowing with the quintrilliant brilliance of worlds beyond worlds—

ELEVEN
THE SHADOW

Then was then. Now is now. With a gulf of years between, not separating but distancing.

It had been a day of summit joy on our ziggurat, our
up-dated "hill-of-heaven," mondeal refuge, called Mount
Heapmore in The Sprawl and if in The Sprawl, then the
world (even The Sprawl is a part of the world. Right?).
There had been festivities on top to celebrate not only
the spring renewal in the plant world but, also, from
within the same living matrix of vitality, the coming of
a new age we felt rising within and around and beyond
us out of some irrepressible spreading leaven. Good vibes
lingered in the dancing air but now the people, from near
and far, had started pouring down the terraces for further
activities below. Sound itself whispered backward and
down with a diminishing babble of voices on the lower
slopes. I must hurry with the bird feed, join the others
in the world room.

Out of the corner of my eye I glimpsed a butterfly
glider dangling high on the larch tree by its hollow struts,
a stranded fugitive from the world of fantastic shapes.

117

Strange about gliding. It could answer all soaring cries like glint from a bird's wing. On the basis of a secret I shall go on, I told myself, glowing in mime's whiteface with stars for eyes. So I still assured myself whenever I came too close to the shadow, that shadow of what in my mind lay just beyond the border, around the corner, as close as two steps yet as unreal as—? A shadow detached from substance and smiling? A moan laid to rest like a stifled song?

Never fear I tried to quiet the old familiar reserve. The shadow had no physical weight but it said something as reassuring as a physical touch: it said clearly that force has no power to hold, that love can reach beyond death.

For a moment I stood gazing out to the far hazy rim of the horizon, beyond the plain, beyond The Sprawl, out to where the whole world, the far circling line between land and sky seemed to circle and spin and circle. It was hot and the world kept turning inside my head in the world of my head. Welcome exhaustion! It was just then, feeling the need for shade that I felt the shadow, a real one, a shadow of substance this time. It came as a sudden touch of coolness on my hot skin, a dash of chill almost, oddly clinging. It was laid across my shoulders like a shawl woven of breezes, hovering above, moving as I moved.

Out of the muted blue a reassuring portent for me?

There was no mystery about this shadow. It was wing shaped, the shade of the right wing across my right shoulder and the shadow of the left on my left.

"Shall we dance?" I called up.

118

I took a few steps and the shadow clung in cadence.

Now that the time had come to celebrate the new age rising within us, now that the very air snapped with promise, had the time not also come to lay to rest that other thing, the frightful, loving, clinging thing? With mercy as sweeping as it was conclusive. Not forgetting of course. That would be abandoning? For the details were forever there. The red of her head scarf, whipped off, shining, streaming, screaming, red like blood. The red of his hair, as curly and unruly as a child's, shorn to the skin like a tethered ram's in a shearing pen, the magnificent skein-of-self discarded with brutal if routine inclusiveness as mere sweepings on a public floor. His oddly gleaming naked head. No, there was no danger I would forget. But I was learning a clear strange truth, little grasped in its deepstem brainstem implications: anguish for close ones can be more painful than sorrow for self. More excruciating. I did not fear a blow to self in the same way I told myself. I could act, I could counter. I could even bounce back! Even rage could explode in a laugh? For myself I could forgive. But for them? In their behalf, that is. The bind was tighter, more enduring. Besides, was not forgiving a matter between victim and violator? For a third one however emotionally involved to intrude, then, would be just that. An intrusion. Inappropriate. Presumptuous.

Yes for them I was more vulnerable than for myself. Lay the unquiet thing to rest? How? Rather must I not grow past it, around it? Like the amber-red crystalline encasement bees build about the stung body of an intruding field mouse, too monstrously heavy to remove from the hive but not too big to contain and immobilize within their busy interior world? To grow past and around, that seemed the answer, the thing preserved airtight but rendered nonthreatening. I should be free, then, like the tireless bees with their paper-fragile abode hanging in the blossomed apple tree, the whole outwardly none the worse and without a visible flaw.

"Come down," I called to the hovering shape above, "who are you?"

I knew of course. But couldn't believe it.

There was, in fact, no mistaking his identity. Only one big bird was that compact and rotund in the center section between port and starboard wings, and also from north to south between the conspicuous ear tufts and the abbreviated tail. The central bulk, the vermiculated ventral expanse, the cunning barrel shape, none of this could pass unrecognized. But why would he venture back to the people zone? Out on a foray had he become directionally confused and lost his way? Never. This big fellow had a built-in map-perfect sense of orientation. Was he, then, the victim of more sensitive pressures, his reappearance spelling belated thanks because we had sprung him free at that crucial time? Of course not. No sane gratitude required a return to the still menacing if once sprung trap that had perpetrated the threat in the first place. But wait. Could the whole thing be explained in a more tender vein? Even—should I be touched?— did he remember me as his make-do mother?

No. Face it. In his bag of priorities that kind of sentiment was not packed on top. Past the necessitous functional stage he had long since nipped that frayed apron string loose with one conclusive snip. Perhaps then—of course—the only explanation to make sense? Could it be? He had lofted back to the danger zone out of something far more portentous, something that of itself and alone would warrant the desperate defiance of diurnal exposure?

Something deep enough to be both blind and driving?

"You're safe here," I sang out a dubious reassurance for the bird and myself, squinting up in his direction.

With a noiseless sweep of fringed pinions he came skimming in on a slant, lifting and sinking as if half blinded in the full light. With no further ado he then winged straight past me into the dim haven of a cone-sweet young fir tree, a special plant protegée. The dark green prickle-tickling fragrant *lifeform* trembled in her sudden role of a welcome shelter for the distinguished guest. His dignity, his spontaneous pomposity, his ponderous if highly sensitive sobriety, all of this the little tree swallowed without a trace within her spreading branches. In a moment I saw his eyes gleaming out like reflectors from the sheltered dark between two boughs, dour yellow in a stare of pure glare.

"If you prefer not to come out, shall I come in?" I asked after a heavy pause.

He held his silence. Except for wavering slits in his huge luminous orbs, his presence held firm.

Slowly I slid under the lowest branch, entering a one tree forest since all within the fir's thick sheltered shade circle gave an illusion of being far off, muffled and privately remote. I sat quietly at the base, all hugged together like I used to sit in the real forest of The Place Where All Things Come Together.

I waited patiently. His bulk stirred above me on a branch halfway up. Why did I sense that his beak was gaping open?

In the long silence my patience began to strain and in the end I sat smarting. So he had no time or heart for a demonstrative welcome. Much less motherhovering. All right. He wouldn't get either. The next move was up to him. It wouldn't be ME who broke the spell.

TWELVE

CARRY THE TIGER
TO THE MOUNTAIN

But it was.

I could still see the owl from the bottom side up through the branches, a fuzzy circle of fluff with hidden claws barely showing as clutch lines on the bough. What was he waiting for? Having driven himself back against the grain was he now finding the thing too much to disgorge, to spew out and have done? And why now, waiting for him to move, did I again have a vivid flash of that thing I had been trying to come to grips with just before he appeared? The thing that began just after I fled the forest that crucial time so long ago when The Place Where All Things Come Together flew apart in my head. At that time, way back then when he was but a fledgling barely able to launch his own wings—and I was The Most Powerful Six-Year-Old in the entire world. Powerful! Powerful?

"After I ran out of the forest," I broke the silence, "do you know—?"

If he wouldn't believe, who would?

Beyond the border, around the corner, as close as two steps—

"She was not lost," I declared. My voice sounded strange to my own ears, "Tranquilli."

Dare I at long last go over that path again? My chest felt tight, I swallowed air. On merciful impulse spew it out, say it all clear and sharp as glass shattered in a pitiless glare of sun? For some other creature ear at last to hear, to absorb the sound of the crash, the break.

"I was out on this path," I plunged on, "a place like on another planet but real, our own planet, true, but strange, a wide flat open space, not all that different when you consider what deserts are, halfway across, deserted, bare, like a bog with all the peat dug out. Water had been there but was all gone except for oozing in some of the deeper cracks, the rest all drained away with everywhere parched rivulet traces like dried tear marks on the face of the earth—"

I paused. I had gone this far. Now I would have to say it all?

"I heard this—*sound*—behind me—"

Above, Orison sighed. Deep. As if pulling the world up on a fraying string—

"I turned. There she was! As whole as life. Except that—"

Overhead the bird barely stirred, shifted, held silent—

"—except that her heart was showing. Through the chest wall. I mean open. You know. Not like those awful pictures. Religious saints and such. But real. Pulsing.

126

Nightmare! I struggled to come out of it. I couldn't breathe, I couldn't move. I couldn't cry out. One saving thing. Strange too. Her face was glowing and happy as if she had been coming over half the world to find me against all odds and now here we were and all was well. I blinked, unfrozen. I looked again. The light had played tricks? The bright red heart on her chest was only a silk heart afterall. Bright red silk in a heart shape pinned on her long dark dress. With white letters US painted on over the red like some kind of sign.

"It's us," I shouted, grasping at a sign in my head. "It's US. We're back—"

At least two of us were back. I put down a stab of doubt. If Tranquilli was there could Mox be far behind?

I turned then to run back to her but she put me off. Her face was still shining, true, embracing me in a glow, yet she gestured for me to stop short. "Turn around Mini," she ordered in a way I had never heard from her before, still smiling, "Look back where you were going. What do you see against the sky?"

It was that strange shape. I had been puzzling at it as I headed for it with no certain place to go. Far off on the horizon. Some kind of mountain? A mountain-sized building? Or in some weird mixmatch way a blend of both? True, there were other things against the horizon. A whole city for one, off on the other side, as great as a mountain range, not just one peak, purple mountains' majesty in concrete and steel. Flanked off there also far across the desiccated plain. A packed people zone, that much was sure.

"The city?" I ventured, knowing I was wrong.

"No. Not the city. *The other*—"

"I see it," I said.

"Go there," she said tersely.

I turned as a new cold knowing permeated, rising as a chill out of the ground in spite of the hot bright sun.

She was still smiling and looking directly at me when she vanished.

*   *   *

The owl sat still for all of it while the rest poured out of itself, all of it, flowing, with no stopping. Yet was I not going over it for myself, for the kind of deliverance that only he in his dimension (both more and less than my own?) would be able to grasp, to appreciate, to *bear*?

This is the way it was: no matter how I trudged the mountain got no closer. As I moved it stood still and I treaded a tread in the middle of a hot barely moving glare. I was dying. Not just for water to drink. But to drown in. With quenching of thirst before quenching of me. Goodby and good riddance but first let me have a drink to swallow and be swallowed in. To the parched God is water? The only one with the long cool answer? Right? The laving mystery of it all revealed in a one true drop of rain, a bead of dew, spray from a waterfall? Even a tear? That too? But my eyes could not spare tears. Tranquilli help me! If you want me to get there help me! Next thing I knew I was in a new kind of jumble, or would you call it a peoplemade jungle? The sprawl of the city reached out even over onto this farther side of the plain and took me in. But now, closer, the mountain shape was gone. Sunk behind a blocking obstacle of broken-tooth roofs and high-humming wires and billboards and other straggling traces of people places. The air was limp, fringe city breath ambient with the stinging drift of dead exhausts and vague chemical stinks mingled with the stale ventings from restaurant fans. Was that a whiff of Carmelkorn? Beautiful! A clear sweet amber current in a polluted stream. Coming from where? There was this curb. On a half-paved kind of street at the petered-out end of the clatter and clutter, with grass growing defiantly in the cracks and with a thin spread of shade under a stunted gingko. I lay down there, how long I don't know, until a boy with a coke came alone on a battered old bike and touched me on the tip of my sandal with the tip of his sneaker to see if I was alive.

"Ya kiddin?" he asked.

"I'm waiting for my twin brother who can't be born now because my mother is dead," I explained.

"Y'kiddin!" he heaved a loud fandangle sigh of relief, "I thought I hadda report a dead body."

"I'm dying for a coke," I said.

He took a parting swig on the bottle and passed it to me. I sat up then and gulped the rest down.

"God is a coke," I told him.

"That's too much," he said, "even Coke wouldn't make that claim. Or would they?" He cocked his head and made a clown face that was perfect.

"You're Andy!" I suddenly recognized him. My one true counter in the act. If he could make the right face who needed a carrot wig, candy stripe hose and dutch bag pants?

"I ain't Andy," he corrected, "I'm Seth."

Seth? Where had I heard that before? The third man. The third son of the originals. Not Cain. Not Abel. But Seth. Not the killer. Not the killed. But the third one, different from both. After the others were gone, to start new—

He read my mind. "Yeh yeh I know," he heaved another huge overdone sigh while making a gesture as if juggling a burden between his shoulders, "Not the murderer—or the murdered, okay? Neither an oppressor old fool nor yet a damn fool counter fool who just sits there and takes it. Right?"

"Neither tromping or tromped on," I cried.

"Neither the cook or the cooked," he agreed. Again he made that face.

"I know what they want of me," he blurted, "they want me to be something they ain't. Then get mad from both sides—"

Now he swung away and began explaining in body talk, showing off a feat of skill, of balance within dynamic tension like on an invisible highwire but using the curb, his arms flung out, tipping, swaying, recovering, not falling, "while they zap from one side and drag from the other."

I watched him retreat down the line, turn with a tight flip twirl, knees momentarily bent to catch and hoist his own weight as on a well centered spring, now again groping with toes hooked into that invisible groove. Slowly he returned with just the right stance as a part not apart from the total suspension. Once more he stood before me as tall as he could make tall. All he needed to finish was a bow. But he just stood there.

I clapped. "Beautiful."

"It's no act," he accused, "can't you see that?"

"Two weights you have to have," I tried to make up, "with only one you'd really be off line."

"Highwire walkers of the world arise," he declared with an edge and no laughs, "you have nothing to lose but your center of gravity."

Abruptly he changed the subject, "You can't stay here forever," he pointed out, impatient to get going.

"Why not?"

"Talk sense. You'll get hungry. Freeze at night. Stuff like that."

"I'm going to the mountain," I remembered, "but it's gone."

"What mountain?"

"The one that was against the sky."

"That? That's no mountain. That's a heap of stuff dollied up. You mean Mount Heapmore?"

"Is that what they call it?"

"You a heapie?"

"What's a heapie?"

"You talk like one and you ain't even been there yet," he persisted, "is it true they got piped-in sunlight in the big ground place?"

"The world room," I informed him. How had I known?

"—through mirrors in tunnels that flash around corners and make shifting waver on the walls?"

"I'll never make it!" I wailed. It was true. I had no legs. To stand on that is. I tried to get up but a swarm of liquid weights shifted in my head and I fell back, "The ground is the best place to be," I shared basic news.

"Yeh I know," he chimed in, "because you can't fall off."

Even from knees kneeling down I couldn't make it. I began to shiver.

"I mighta known," he groaned, "get on!"

He had taken off his shirt and wadded it across the rear carrier of the bike for a padded buddy seat, "Okay. Quit making like torture. It's easier to take you than to tell you especially if you can't walk."

He had to help me on and I lay like a limp shirt across his sweaty back, my hands clasped tight around his belly. I looped off then except for keeping awake just enough to hang on as we bumped over streets or roads or fields or parking lots or whatever for—how long? The sun was beginning its long slide down to greet the *yin* when we ran into a cool place with suddenly freshened air. I opened my eyes. We were on a green path with no buildings in sight except a cupola over one tree. "Witchamocka County Zoo," Seth said, "some of the animals got moat habitats but most are still jailed for offenses they never done, even juveniles. Pythons they claim got only lunk feelings but they're better off than most. They got their own pit with

132

sun and shade for a choice." Now he was shivering. "I had a raccoon buddy escaped from here once," he went on, pedaling hard up a slight incline, "Greatfeller. He used to ride in the basket up front and sleep on my bed. But he got love sick and run off to the swamp before they drained it to look for a mate."

"What happened to him after they drained his place?" I asked, heavy inside with a parched barren vision.

"Who only knows," he was quick to answer, "in a place I hope free an' okay. When they're wild you gotta let 'em go y'know. They gotta live their own lives—"

Now we burst out onto another plain, a shallow saucer of wide earth, the park shrubs and border bushes, the windbreak of poplars all dropping behind us. I peeked out over Seth's shielding shoulder—*and there it was*. O! I hid my face as if struck in the eyes by a glancing apparition. Dare I look again? It was still there, real in an unreal way, the earth itself heaved up in a solid bulk dream, bearing down on us yet floating, seeming to twirl in the day's dying glow yet shafting that glow as if rooted in the weight of the world. There it was, the unimaginable materialized, a cometrue ziggurat hanging garden, solid enough to douse the sun yet with a persistent golden aura flowing along all its horizon terraces. Seeming to be earth out of earth with its fringes of growth, yet clearly fashioned by hands and minds out of visual insistence, it stood there at once defiant and inviting, an enormous pulse of assertion both heavy and shimmering.

How close, how far? Distance glimmered in its own

mirage. A long way yet close, farflung yet near, its mag-
nitude seemed magnified out of all proportion through a
small lense of awe. Awe—or fear?

"I'm no longer Mini," I said, cold.

Who would I be when I got there?

Mount Heapmore, the real, was coming up fast; now
it seemed everywhere. Apart from the fact that its sheer
strangeness seemed to achieve a sort of ethereal intim-
idation, its solid realness had to be dealt with. *Who can
appreciate even beauty in the face of fear?* Here at last
was the new fright full destination I had said I wanted
to reach, a suddenly devouring destination from which
all others dropped away, all the dear and familiar of the
past flung away for this unknown, the past itself spun
out into space as spent and already gone. Goodby but not
good riddance—*don't think I'll forget* DON'T THINK I'LL
ever FORGET. Was there no turning back?

Movement flowed forward relentlessly, smoothly.

"Chicken?" asked Seth.

"I have to follow the link," I said weakly.

"You still Mini?"

"Okay. Mini."

It was true. At least I still had me.

I clung on tight once more and closed my eyes.

"There's no need," now Seth began to lay it on, "to be
scared. They're all harmless y'know. They make a big
thing'a it. Not t'hurt. Like it was something they in-
vented. With kites in the sky."

"DM," I recognized, "*dynamic harmlessness.*"

A low but wide-arched opening, not a door, not even

134

a special fancy portal, was coming into view, beginning to take shape. And there were people. Human shapes. What else? Also, as we came closer, at least one donkey, a pair of bleating goats, plus a couple of dogs one of whom, a huge boxer with a glowering mug sat there alert with a tiny kitten asleep over one ear. The people made way for our rolling wheels as if there were nothing unusual in the scene and someone said hi. Seth came with me to the opening although, still weak in the knees, I found I could walk again by myself. At the entrance, looking in, he seemed to develop telescope sight as he peered into the cavernous chamber, squinting and intense.

"Come in and stay with us," I invited.

"Not now," he said, "I got people who'll miss me. Stuff like that—"

"Another day?"

"Another day."

I headed, then, for a sleeping bag that was lying in a neat depression in the the stone floor, actually as it turned out, in the sunken claw mark of an horrific monster. I fell down exhausted, unafraid, and went to sleep.

THIRTEEN
DREAM CLOTH

The path was wide and shimmering, spangled and shifting of colors as of a spectrum in moist light. Do other planets have rainbows? Of course. Some at least. Those in our own dimension? It was the colors I craved as hunger and thirst. I bathed in all of them in turn and then plunged from one to another, blue mini, red mini, purple mini, yellow mini with a green mini whose orange hair had a halo of green; aureoles within aureoles, auras beyond auras, tints cooly boiling and melting within tints, weeping blending shaded within fluid tints and shades, with flashes of shattered luminescence as bright as exploding astonishment. Was I seeing the unseeable? I knew this was a dream. I was not deceived. But there is the waking real and the dreaming real and why should I not glory and shriek for as long as it lasted? Do not fade dreams! Do not desert me! Where is glory as glorious as dread is dreadful? Here was the touchable and breathable and feelable more keen than in any waking scene. I floated up the arched way high over all with no fear of falling. Was I flying or had the path begun to soar up and away,

139

arching now toward what seemed infinity? Was I flying, floating or simply being borne along? No need here for underlying arms to break a fall or a life net to catch for here was the point of balanced suspension, of equilibrium between forces, the libration point. That much was clear. I cascaded down the face of a niagara of cerise, looped a loop in the foam and with a mere arch of my back where wings should be floated back up to enjoy the view. I was still thirsty. Why couldn't I shake that thirst? This was supposed to be perfect, a peep into paradise, yet here was this terrible thirst again. The blue! Blue to slack thirst. I dived, I immersed and, unquenched, surfaced in the blue air. I plunged into the blue again on a band as wide as sight, all the blues shifting and fading and then again flaring like an icy aurora with streamers, borealis bands, curtains and arcs reflecting infinite auroras. Was that an iceberg floating this way, heavenly aquamarine, translucent, burning as cold as fire burns hot? I stuck my tongue out to welcome it with a lick and swallowed a merciful sliver of something that burned cold all the way down. But now I was cold. Shivering. Getting numb? Go for the violet and beyond plunge into the warmer purple. Taste the purple. Grapes? Grapes running with juice as a mighty river? Drink! Drink! Too sweet. Too dark. A dark dry velvety taste to purple. No good for thirst. Smothering too. I gasped for air. Now I knew it as clear as clarity is clear. Only lemon yellow would quench: in the whole of being, out of all time and sense is there anything that can take the place of a lemon except the pure marvel of a living lemon? But I would have to go through the red, then the orange with their too real flaring and flaming. I cringed. Why should I fear red? I loved red. It was a brave color, orange too, the closest thing to the sun at noon. I swam in, cautious. Could I take it? Swimming in the sun? Relax. Remember this was a dream. The pain was not real. True, the orange proved worse than the red for sheer consuming. But now it was fading, blending into the luminous edge of the yellow, pure cooling yellow. Frosty even? Love me!

I felt a slap across my forehead. It was cold. Icy cold. I tried to open my eyes but a wet cloth, dripping with frigid spring water, had been laid across my forehead and was dripping down over my face, my neck, my chest; my arms and legs too felt cold and weighted.

"Fever's not down," someone said, "keep going."

"Lemon," I cried.

The edge of a spoon was in my mouth. Lemon water with honey. I sipped. I tried to gulp.

"One sip at a time," said the voice, cool, mellow, commanding in a fluid way.

Now a slapping slosh of cold was laid on one thigh. I stirred. I remembered where I was. I was helpless, a prisoner in a monster's claw, tied down like Gulliver among who knows what, immobilized under weights of wet cloths, ringed by voices and orders. I peeped out under the cloth on my forehead. They were mere children, my own age or little older, some even younger, several thumbsucking toddlers mingling among the rest. Yet the voice with the lemon spoon was older, melodious but true to the point with no trills to spare. I could see only her long billowing

141

skirt and her movement as the spoon again reached my lips.

"She's awake," one of them said over my right ear, "she's coming to—"

I sighed as someone lifted the cloth off my head and then I saw her for the first time, Luz Marina, towering above, a tall black woman who looked like she had swallowed a piece of the rainbow and it was glowing from the inside out.

"Hi honey," she said, "more honey?"

"Water," I said. I licked the drips off my face.

"Water it'll be," she agreed, "but only a sip at a time."

That again. I tried to gulp. I remembered something Mox had told me: when the colors of the rainbow are all blended together they glow in transparency as in a crystal—or air, or water. Water, pure, then is as precious as a sparkling chunk of diamond by magic turned to liquid. *That's* what I wanted to reach in all my travels, that's what this was all about. "W a t e r!" I cried. They were wrong. Gulps were good, not bad. "WATER!" I wailed.

Luz brought a cup then but cautioned, "Slow. Take it slow."

I gulped.

I've been inside a rainbow, I marvelled, but I've come back to life for a drink of water!

"What can you do that's good for something?" asked a bold gaunt brown boy. He was sitting knob-kneed and cross-legged beside me, enormous intense sober eyes taking in all the action.

"Shut up Heyzoos," reproached a plump pink chub of

142

a girl, "What you expect from someone dying?" She cupped a dimpled paw over my left ear and apologized for his audacity, "He's a genius brain damaged from *hunger infantitus*. We're trying to feed him back into normal. Pay no mind."

"I don't mind," I answered.

"What can you do?" Heyzoos persisted, still intense, insistent.

For a moment everything stopped. One by one they took me in as, sitting, squatting, standing, they ringed me, all looking down as I lay there in their midst.

O! Should I tell them my secret, declare my bright gift? For one moment I had an impulse to pour out the unbelievable in a rush, with whole trust. But no! Let them discover it as I had discovered it. I smiled back without words but with a whole wide world of expectation. Then Luz clapped her hands and a cheer went up from around the circle.

It was natural, of course, that I should become bird feeder on the summit, a joy to behold.

FOURTEEN

BIRDS DON'T

HAVE TO BE FRISKED

Luz Marina. Light-of-the-Sea. "why do you have my mother's other name?" I asked point blank because I had to.

Luz appeared stopped, astounded. "Child, because it is me," she declared, "In–did–gee–nous. Remember that. Never forget it. In–did–gee–nous."

Of course. She was born in the islands where the palms bend east with the winds, where the river in the sea flashes aqua and streams toward the rising day underneath a never ceasing river of air. "In mild gracious water as pure as a baby's tear I floated before I could crawl," was her boast, "I could swim three ways before I could walk." And the pearl. The lucky find, was that true, the breath-holding dive at only age six? Six like me, like I was then. The enormous perfect pearl, growing every time the tale was repeated, she never claimed yes, she never claimed no. And so the legend stood.

That was Luz Marina, granddaughter of Nitti Gritti the Original, the elder legendary one who, striving to complete a dream, died within shouting distance of the

147

summit. For me missing pieces began to fall into place. It was he, Nitti, who had first come to a lost strange place, the site of the old abandoned New Jersey dinosaur trample area, a centrally avoided no-person's land that was actually the dried up bed of a Mesozoic water hole. It was he Nitti, I learned, who had been an independent solid waste specialist who, approaching with his battered but sturdy old dump truck, first refused to place any of the reduced compacted G-T (garbage-trash) blocks over the paleozoologically significant petrified ex-creature foot pads and, instead, systematically dumped, more like built around them, creating a foundation line of sorts. Caught up in a vision to build for the ages to match the tread of the past, from then on it was a case of dumping up, never down. Eventually with a ground level central chamber, grand in a strange sort of way, a fitting world chamber really, arched over and reinforced through a smart system of interlocking parts on a jigsaw principle, they told me, with all parts mutually locking in stronger and stronger as the stress overhead increased. Something on the principle of a natural cave and featuring within, naturally, the monstrous dragon if now harmless time-frozen tootsie marks. Lit at first only with lightning bugs, eventually the pioneers tried to convert to lightning power *per se* but found 2×10^{11} joules per bolt somewhat jolting to handle even with clever do-it-yourself grounding. Long since the ecocommunity, then, went over to a safe, clean, endlessly renewing wind-powered and solar culture. With a bonus. A gift from old Hera. A reestablished spring in the midst, one claim being that the weight of the great mass of Mount Heapmore reactivated spigots not active since the thunder lizards last came to drink.

And Luz? She too was a mover for it was she who moved that community decisions be made at ground level in a circle among all, all those affected by the decision a part of the decision. With the top reserved strictly for the birds.

*   *   *

They knew it all, what happened to Mox and Tranquilli. Was there some kind of mind planted in the vitals of the magic heap?

Actually the thing could be explained without astral help. A company of guerrilla theatre anti-warriors had come by Mount Heapmore for commiseration and refreshments and, still smarting from a rough confrontation, spilled over with the particulars of an heroic and crazy witness, tragic, fatal in fact for one, a heavy jail snare for a second (a mere bystander, how ironic can you get?), plus the usual normal harassment for all the others. Added to all this, Luz remembered who we were from a few years back and identified the casualties in the drama: "Pacha Mama!" she had cried at the time, "I know who you're talking about. The child? At least we must find the child."

To me now, precipitously arrived for refuge in their midst, she said, "We were searching for you and you've found us."

Then she surprised me with this further news, "You've been here before," she declared, "can you remember back

149

so far? You were a diapered bébé and already balancing high over your papa's head in a straight true kneelock, all natural and sassy, baby feet flat on his supporting hands, with your mama circling to catch—just in case—with her arms held out in a swaying cradle—"

I tried to think back.

It was all dim, actually a blank. A blank within a circling place that one might fall into with walls of voices and arms made of—*anxious eyes*? Eyes as deep as a swirling place in a world opened up, then the earth closing and rising and closing again in a fold of soft-yielding yet firm-holding arms. Beautiful world! Without wings one can cast oneself into the blue, confident, sailing, laughing, always to be caught with screams of joy.

But a lingering imprint persisting through endless scenes is not remembering as they meant it.

"It was on the day before Nitti died," Luz persisted, lost now in her own remembering, "at age 100. Within shouting distance of the top while we were all still a-building. The day the sun buttons, dandies in swarms and millions, all burst out on the lower slopes where earth fill was spread. A wild ringing spill of gold, shrieking with yellow. Pax and Tranquilli came by to help us celebrate Nitti's centennial—"

"He's no longer Pax. He's Mox," I corrected.

"Pax or Mox, he's in jail," said Apple, the plump ruddy one.

"For food maybe," added Heyzoos, "they threw him the book."

150

"For not having a piece of teeny cardboard, imagine," embellished Apple.

"Size two centimeters by three," reinforced Heyzoos, "printed to kill."

Mox was alive? The question I had dared not ask even to myself. Locked up, maybe. But alive? An unquiet weight, crying inside, dropped away. I breathed as if for the first time. I gulped air as I had gulped water. They had not abandoned me then. I knew it. I had known it all along. Stumbling in myself. But only a little. For a moment I continued to lay there taking it in as a feeling of familiar realness returned, rising up all around me as out of some far calling center. "He's alive," I put it into words cautiously, carefully, little more than a whisper. Suddenly, then, on impulse, I included them all in tears. Free flowing. Copious. O yes the tears. A fountain, a living gushing fountain and I was the source. Their little arms were all around me, hugging, patting. Those who could not get close tried to reach out and touch me.

Then a new bolt struck, reality too, and no longer balm. "They can't keep him in a cage," I cried, "he'll—he'll—"

He'll—*what*?

I was up now on my knees, struggling to stand up.

"Take it easy," cautioned Luz Marina, an arm around my waist as she helped me to my feet, "remember we are not helpless."

"We aren't?" Another weight fell away inside.

"Never!" she avowed. "First we must get word to him that you are found, that you are not lost."

Of course. Mini is alive Mox never fear! Was he getting the thought waves right now? At this very moment?

"Now he can stop his hunger fast," said Heyzoos, "and start eating the macaroni. They got it in big vats y'know, big as a bathtub." The boy was smacking his lips with shameless relish.

"We can plant a tree," offered Apple, "a little shoot."

"A Mini shoot," corrected Heyzoos.

"Outside the main gate of the prison—" Now they were all talking.

"—under the big wall where the pigeons perch—"

—to run messages—"

"—without getting shot at."

"Birds don't have to be frisked through the metal detectors—"

"—for beeps—"

"—like people do—"

"—sail right over the walls—"

"—flop down neat into The Yard."

"Plop."

"Strut."

"With no sweat."

FIFTEEN

IRON BACK HAND

They knew it all. Too vivid. Too real. The big thing was that Tranquilli had burst her bounds, had stepped out of herself to come to get me. But with Mox trapped back at the scene.

They were on the way to get me, that much was clear, to return to The Place Where All Things Come Together, progressing through distance, running in their minds. Everything had taken too long but now they were coming. What stopped them was this: they ran into this guerrilla theatre in a town square passing through. They had to stop to feed and rest Him and Her, our donkey pair who pulled our caravan with its brand new exterior mural of Titmouse on the Sistine. Why not, then, see someone else's act at the same time? A ghastly thing. As bad as a real life accident. Terrible on purpose. All spread out beneath this great soaring memorial monument, everyone knows the kind, liberty spreading her stone wings high over all against a blue sky, her shadow shielding the bronze plaque on which was engraved the long columns of the names of the brave and honored dead of past wars. A grand place for open theatre, boards of the world, the proscenium the arch of the sky. They're in damn rotten taste someone shouted, they ought to be arrested. One woman shopper shielded her child's eyes as she hurried by. My God I'm against the war she said but this is sickening. Why can't they just write to the editor or Congress or something? All over the plaza steps was frozen mayhem, a tangled fall of bloody flesh and torn black pajamas and strewn conical straw hats, bare arms, naked feet, the bodies, some face up with staring eyes, some grotesque and twisted face down but all smeared with heavy viscous red stuff. Not real blood of course. For a backdrop a big banner said YOUR TAX DOLLARS AT WORK and down front was another smaller sign carried by a young mother in pigtails with her own small kid, a flaxen haired boy clinging onto her jeans and whining to go home. Their sign said

it costs the
military
$189,918
to
maim or kill
an Asian
woman and child

Jeff be still said the young mother remember you promised to do your part for your Asian sisters and brothers. On the top step under the big banner in the middle of all was a towering Spectre of Death, I mean tall, so tall he had to be on stilts under his black robe, with skeleton

156

hands and a globular skull mask with live eyes shining out. A tableau. Everything silent. Everything still. No movement. No sound. The wax works in flesh. Or like a picture caught still from the evening news in living color. Red, white and black. Anti-war. The whole thing was anti-war. Get it?

It was a down trip all the way. Mox didn't get involved, a matter of the code. He wouldn't cut in on someone else's act, right? But Tranquilli, wouldn't you know, got carried away on the basis that this was real life and not a mere act. Watching, she started to cry, then had to do instead of mere be. It was then that she whipped off her red silk head band, clipped it into a heart shape and pinned it onto her chest. Then she began wringing her hands out front on the public walk, as regal and beautiful as Lady MacBeth in her long dark dress, miming and grieving like the conscience of the nation. She's the troubled conscience of the nation Mox explained to a woman standing next to him who looked him over without a word and then moved away. It was at that moment that the Spectre of Death crooked a finger at Tranquilli as much as to say come up and join us and next thing there she was, now with a big white u.s. chalked on her red silk heart, soundlessly wailing and weeping and wringing her hands among all those live corpses, the only accent of movement in the scene.

The crowd? That's where the trouble was. Torn. Not like cloth torn but like something living with nerve ends strained ready to rip, both sides hurting as they parted and accused, faces at once veiled and stony, staring, turn-

157

ing away, some flushed with anger or—what?—a few laughing but not laughing. Someone has to jolt us alive someone said to face the real thing. Freaks someone else said, pure freaks. What kind of people can they be willing to sprawl if not naked almost as bad on the public street? Carnography is worse than pornography any day said a tall lank clean-cut fellow clicking away with his camera from every angle. Tell 'em to go get an honest job bellowed another fellow out of a car as he careened around a corner, squealing to a slowdown to make his blast. Then things took a turn. If we can't take even this much what of our real victims mildly queried a sober egg-shaped old woman with a sassy salt-and-pepper dutch-boy bob, a peace sign locket dangling with no apologies down over her smooth but copious bosom. Was it her low-key but pointedly unilateral inference that broke the storm? OUR roared a stentorian voice worthy of a beleaguered commandant, OUR?!, madam, what about THEIR repeat THEIR victims? BE HONEST you damn peaceniks, always putting down our own, what about THEIR horrors? DOCUMENTED! Including OUR OWN men getting it right now, RIGHT NOW getting killed THIS VERY MINUTE AS we stand here TAKING THIS—@¢/! A plain middle-aged woman nearby stood as if transfixed, trembling, lost in herself, her face working fighting tears, until the man with her put a burly arm over her shoulder to draw her away: you don't need anymore of this Mom. They can't dishonor Ralph, he was no killer—

Was it the first stone or the police whistle that signalled all hell loose? Both seemed to come at once. The first stone, a sharp gravel fleck that first one, striking Jeff on the forehead, a small gash but drawing real blood, the frantic whistle, the young mother throwing her poncho over the child then raising her head in an involuntary cry, face distorted, peace! peace! she screamed can't you see we want peace? A shudder passed over the corpses but, disciplined, they remained prone, limp on principle, taking the pelting: remember, whatever is thrown at you hold onto this *the victims you are proxy for have suffered far worse.* Now the police swarm among them, kicking a few to arouse them, pushing the crowd back to make way for the wailing wagon. What have we done said a corpse raising his head, we're unarmed. We've got a permit for a nonviolent demo protested another. The missiles aren't coming from us pointed out a third. We're protecting you said the cop, towering over, it's out of hand, come along, no resistance. We resist said the first corpse, once more limp, his head back down on the concrete step, now plugged into mental gravity with a sensitive spot in the middle of his forehead plumblining the center of the earth. You're arrested said the cop for resisting arrest. Drag me by the shoulders if you would please instructed the glued-down corpse I've got a tender scalp.

Does anyone *know* what it is for even a pair of husky troopers to try to lift a body dead weight when that body is plugged into *mental gravity*?

No problem, of course, with the Spectre of Death. He was an easy mark on his stilts and he went sailing— thwack!—with a rush to his underpinnings. CLEV-ER! Off he went in an arc, landing as if on springs, palms and elbows flexible as he rolled with the blow like a skilled acrobat—*or a trained combatman?* His wild maché mask split open but absorbed the crash like a helmet. O o p s! Up he popped out of the shattered shell, a young longhair, what else? You were expecting, maybe, General Westmoreland? But hold. He WAS a soldier. Hurrah! Raise the flag? A real one. An ex-combatman, yet, in his own fatigues with a purple heart dangling and obvious as some kind of statement.

God help us someone said. Was the earth opening in a crack? From the beginning whoever heard—

Tranquilli, actually, was the first one in the paddy wagon. Wandering around free and conspicuous an officer simply picked her up bodily over his shoulder and deposited her neatly. It was Mox's intervention that portended the portentous, the first fateful step in the fatal downbeat. You can't take her he challenged she's not with them. Whadda ya mean countered the law on eyeball evidence she's the main thing. If you take her you take me too insisted Mox; be my guest said the law.

Not carrying a draft card, that's how they nailed him. Or rather for not having one in the first place. Never *intending* to have one in either the first or last place?

All the others they merely cleared off the street and mostly let go after a token hold. But Mox, no, he was stuck, chained to one unyielding fact. Cleared by the civil authorities but held for the military authorities, that was the leg-hold trap he ran into or rather that, this time, with caution flung to the hounds of hell, he himself had walked into.

The hidden clamp, the bone-deep bite, the bleeding hold: a man can't chew his own leg off like a maddened animal can he?

His defense? His first point was routinely preposterous of course. A hidden insult—or a joke? Just his harmless wise fool bit, Uncle's loyal but cheeky jestor? A citizen of Planet Earth hence under the jurisdiction of God-aloneknowswhat. His second point, however, was not only logic tight but unassailable: how can you register for the draft in your own home district like the law says when you have no home district?

Are you a conscientious objector asked the appointed defense looking for a peg; hell no said Mox cooking his own able-bodied gander I'm a c.o. all right, a congenital objector.

No one can say they were not fair. No sense of humor, granted. But fair. A generous offer even? One last chance to kill or be killed without prejudice or penalty, the past by-passed. A second chance at unpenalized impressment with the usual gamble, anything possible all the way up to 4F? For Mox a backhand clutch at deliverance via the knuckledown way? Stocky, blooded, muscled, but with some hidden but hopeful rejection factor to fall back on? Like, say, a head not screwed on right?

Who would ever know? But no. Something was not balanced, something was off center. Congenital objector was where it was at. Anything less was short of a toe hold.

Was Mox running now on some private inner track, adrenalin a dangerous running mate? Had he forgotten

161

that he was a mime of all time, the court-type place but a stage from which to blow them all away helplessly crippled with cracked-up laughter as in a crazy carnival dream? Why did he not simply acupuncture them in all their control points with sticking needles of stupendous earth-changing mirth? As it was there, it seemed, he stood as if already dead in both legs and head. Until with a deft flick, eyelash quick

he stood on his

head.

In their midst, marionette stiff and ram proper, a body at attention in flip posture, still warm but p
e
r
p
e
n
d
i
c
u
l
a
r
l
y
perversely
up side
down.

* * *

The sentence for the too-clever clown did not reflect the humor of the situation

* * *

It all struck fast. Tranquilli, separated with the women in a holding pen (one big cage for all pending processing) heard first that Mox was released and heaved a sigh; it would soon be over, her pen sisters comforted her. No civil charge for that one. Give credit. Justice had peeked out of her blind and distinguished tit from tat. Then the postscript along the rumorous grapevine. No civil charge pressed true but he, the brother with the great mahogany colored hair and freckled neck, the one just passing through who had jumped in for no reason except to put an arm around the Soul of the u.s., for Mox as he called himself the news was not good. A street actor like them, he said, as a matter of professional cooperation and patriotic rapport had been turned over by the city police to the local military authorities to explain his status. Tranquilli stood numb. *Why hadn't their survival signals steered them clear?* Had the time come to weep, to be torn? Why, suddenly, abruptly, had they been drawn to what was now revealed as that dread dreamwork threat, the abyss, deceptively covered over with a web of circumstances so fine and intertwined that on the surface it appeared to offer solid footing?

A real haul, a rare catch. Beside no draft reg. & cat. proof, no other proper identification either including, would you believe, not even a social security number? If not

163

vagrant as he denied, on the face of it a clear cut bona fide d.d. With his attitudes not exactly the most hopeful as a potential complete but useful at least as an example. Right turn. An example to all those other crazies.

In turn, to save the fragments of the saveable if only Tranquilli had kept calm. Did she not know that the one thing society will not tolerate is screaming out of control? It universally sets teeth on edge, shatters all response except retaliatory panic, makes tremble the very foundations. Calm, collected, cool, she at least would have been, it's assumed, turned loose after at most one night in the lockup in lieu of the token fine like all the others, established justice getting her tweak of flesh. But no. Hearing this, hearing that, knowing nothing for sure, trapped in the sweaty milling confines of the cage with her old claustrophobic trouble rising she began, slowly at first, to weave and moan. For herself and her close ones. That was the crux. The pinning to the tree. For herself and for her breath-and-bread ones, her life mate, her helpless child. Helpless? Precocious, true. As wise as a waxing moon in a clear sky, three jumps ahead of January, a boon friend of April. But too tender in her bones yet to experience abandonment, the cold hand that lets go—

"Mox!" Tranquilli called through the bars into the sterile corridor, clean even of visible guards, blazing in a flood light, "Mox! Mox! Where is Mox?"

The door at the end, the electronically secured escape hatch, the only egress out to humanity, was entirely metal and painted a gleaming new green: it only opened on signal, no keys. A new jail, one of her pen sisters told her, a thin young person still clad in torn black pajamas with her make-up gore only partially swabbed off forehead and cheeks. A brand new jail, hardly used, still spic and span, designed strictly for progress, functional. It was true. Functional for what? Who? In one corner of the big pen was a lidless toilet and also a tiny cold water sink, amenities for a crowd, otherwise nothing, only two benches, no other seats, no place to sit except on the concrete floor. The room-sized cage was set down like a giant birdcage inside a still larger flood-lit room, resulting in an illusion of corridors on three sides, the barred area flush against only one wall. It's useless to pound on the bars another trapped sister told Tranquilli, try the wall it's a one-way observation window for the matron or guards.

Now Tranquilli went before the eyeglass window and pleaded her case. There were human beings on the other side she told herself and she addressed the blank slightly frosty-looking grey wall. If human they must have that spark inside. Before giving way to panic she would be reasonable like they liked it, she would appeal, an appeal no one could resist, one to one, or even one to three, whoever was back there. "I have a child," she began reasonably, "who I must go to. She's back at our home place, true no street address but a true place. Take my word. Where is Mox Mutchinson, the one with the great mahogany red hair? We are married by our own way. Ever since the day the Canada geese got confused by radar or something and landed on the green goddess of freedom, all around her crown and up her torch. A good omen for us. But was it okay for the birds? Please! Hear what I am saying! Let me go. Let Mox go. We are needed free where we should be. What have we done? Tell me. Who have we hurt? Who have we killed? Who have we stolen from? No! *No*. We have hurt no one! Not even a scratch! We have taken from no one! Not even a penny! What law have we broken? No! We have broken no law that makes sense. Help us! Help us now! Because if you do, if you do, if you help us I will promise you something greater than you greater than me. I promise you love itself will love you, a true thing poured out for you—"

The blank wall, the knowing window, stared back at Tranquilli.

SIXTEEN

ESCAPE

In the end they called in the police physician, a graying but vigorous old man in a plain business suit, a veteran of years of coping in his own way with the most desperate and volatile eruptions of those whom society had unceremoniously braked to a halt. In short he was the Public Health Officer empowered to commit an inmate or detainee on the spot for emergency attention If The Situation So Warranted, i.e. the latter judged the classic danger to self and/or others.

The needle quieted her enough to get the restraining camisole tied on with the efforts of two animated white coats plus the matron but the effect seemed vaporing off even as she was whisked away on a rolling pallet down through the establishment's own underground, a maze of tunnelled interlinking passages several blocks long underneath and between the Public Safety Building housing courts and jail and the Public Service Complex housing psychiatric units, outpatient clinics and welfare offices. Diagnosis: *disturbed*. Prognosis: *guarded*. Through a fog-bound tempest she recalled only the flash of white tiled walls as they started the roll down a ramp, the rolling rhythm for a moment strangely soothing but as if unhinged, floating, detached. One could not feel a surge of wild assurance in the midst of agony, that was crazy as if at last she had touched the bottom, the true bottom, bitterly testing the underlying basis that would not yield further. At one point midway along on the bumping swaying journey for one flash moment she came starkly awake and aware, visually marking a metal door, hanging there like a picture out of a dream. It had a peep slot and a neat oblong name plate that said pistol range. The whole scene at a dizzy angle passed over her head to one side; then once again came a dive down a ramp, this time into semi-darkness both damp and dusty as they gained the intermediate passages under the central steam plant among coils of huge conduits, several with pressured seams oozing, weeping puddles on the concrete floor.

*　*　*

When Tranquilli had gotten into tight spots before, when—physically—everything seemed to close in, walls constricting as in a blacked-out elevator, a bus trapped in a gassy traffic-packed tunnel, the insane time she had been lured into the twisting stygian crawlway at Timeless Caverns, she had learned a certain technique to free herself; giving way to the rising inner madness would be suicide and she was not then yet ready to die. True, in the cavern crawlway she had had to keep crawling but suddenly on what seemed her own impulse she had been visually freed into a wide meadow, smelling the damp earth instead of the dank cave, unaccountably calm and detached, seeing and urging her fainting body on to deliverance. In the elevator while several others moaned and at least one shrieked it was a case of retreating far back into beginnings, tranced, head hanging down, body crouched, feeling the sensations of life before birth, unconsciously waiting for rebirth through a clanged-open door. The traffic tunnel? No problem. That was transitory. The bus suddenly started up, all was moving again, all was well. Now, however, all that was changed. This trap was of dimensions far beyond the merely physical. Here others were not working to free and rescue. Here others were part of the trap, the walls themselves made of flesh and blood, of blocking bodies that seemed of incomprehensible coldness and hate. Why? What was wrong? Now it was will against will with them holding the key. When she woke up, then, supine on a mattress on a hard floor, spreadeagle in five-star exhaustion, at first disoriented, alone in a cell-like room with padded walls and only a trace of light, she had no illusions: the worst, she grasped with a confirming jolt, had happened. All those passing ones, all those out there who were complacently a part of the way things were, all those who even with laughs they could never quite reach, those, the same, had finally closed in as they had long threatened to do. To stamp out, to destroy. *Why? To stamp out all those who are different?* That was their crime, she and Mox. She saw it clearly. They were different. A crime that could never be forgiven, never reprieved, guilty as charged. An avalanche had blocked the tunnel. The el-

171

evator was not only blacked-out but falling. The cave walls after a million years were collapsing this very minute. Should she give way to screaming once more? Never. Every bit of energy, of strength, of living essence, would be needed for what she instinctively accepted. This was the showdown with not even a crack for a toe hold. But there was still one move. Had they forgotten? Calm. Keep calm. In silence, inert, she had fled to the center, the center of self but far more than self, the center of time, of being, of all that is, known and unknown. For the strength that is like an immersion, for the seeing that must pierce all blinds, for the release that must burst all strictures. Yes there was still one move. Beyond all holding traps there was still one way out to mercy, one way out to the archway, to light. The one way none could block, none control.

Outwit them, cheat them out of that which they could not hold?

Tranquilli was beyond sensation except for a sense of lifting, of lightness: it was happening. Mox. Go first to Mox. See. Find out. Then to the small one. Quickly. Again she closed her already closed eyes. She visualized the real as it happened. It was in no way a case of will but more like a hyper-vivid construct of inner sight, a giving way to assurance at the eyebright center of all assurance: out, out, *out*; the passage was narrow like birth but, like birth, not unyielding, the walls pulsing, a warm flooding sensation, a new kind of love. Once out of the trap, unbound, she could not orient herself immediately as to

172

direction to go to Mox but that proved unnecessary; she saw him, detail for detail, sitting on the side of a bunk in a cell, hands buried in his hair. She tried to touch him but found that his hair no longer had substance and when he looked up briefly it was as if he were blind. It was then and then alone that she felt the pang of parting. A strong surge beyond words, a sense of freed consciousness that sent even what he would call grief tumbling before it. Skimming the miles was as nothing, direction a gateway not a distance. She knew that the small one would not be at The Place Where All Things Come Together yet was drawn there. Needing to retrace, to retrieve, to regain, to assert the lost assurance for this one for who she had been a primal link to assurance? A fledgling owl, soundless, skimmimg, all but winged her, heading straight for her out of the trees, tipping to one side at the last moment as if aware of her presence. Yes it was true. He was aware. How good to communicate without words! She needed no clues yet the clues of the child's retreat from what had been a sanctuary were as a blazed trail, the imprints of passage invisible yet obvious within her new seeing, over the fallen logs, along the mossy way, dodging here and there among the toadstools and Indian pipes, retracing because she had a persisting need to retrace every step to erase the trail of disbelief, of panic in the absence of love. Bursting out finally onto the hot flat plain, the dredged swamp.

There she was.

Now.

But now.

What did *now* longer mean with time itself blended and folding?

Now for one reason only. The small one, in her own sense of timing, must be told. Above all she must be sent in the right direction.

But how could it be done? To speak to be heard by *ear*? To gather all that could be gathered to be seen by *eye*?

How?

How could it be done?

One last effort—

One last task—

A visualization beyond all visualizations—

* * *

Back at the detention unit of the psychiatric hospital they were recording, duly, that the detained one had died of natural causes.

A burst *aortic aneurism* is a natural cause.

Right?

SEVENTEEN
THE CELEBRATION

When my father came out of prison on what was called the first "amnesty" (a clanged-open reduction of time for certain categories) he was changed. I cannot say how. I only know he was different. For one thing Titmouse was gone. When he looked at me I knew he no longer saw Titmouse the endeared cunning one. That was no wonder for I had become a skinny nine-year-old with shoulder blades as bony as vestig wings. A feast had been prepared at our mondeal refuge with balloons to release to the wide earth which said welcome Mox, but he walked into the world room and when he looked around he did not seem to see certain obvious things for what they were. What I mean is his response to the unrestrained celebration seemed less of rejoicing for him than it did for those around him. He was almost like one who emerges from a dark place blinking, deliberate in his reach for enough orientation to feel his way. Thrust to the front as his closest one, I suffered shrinking pangs. It was as though a covering had been stripped off and on the spot I had to improvise a part that was far beyond me. I felt keenly his apparent sense of exposure on the one hand and the high expectations of the wellwishers on the other. For any of various obscure reasons the hero did not readily accept his role?

Everyone knows that when a great soul for a great cause goes to prison or is somehow confined, bound in, restricted, deprived not only of freedom but of painfully much more, that one, that purged one, refined and unfaltering, comes out stronger not weaker. No matter what horrid hell is cooked up the inspired enduring one emerges to cry out the liberating truth. And so sets a banner in the sky.

So it is. So it does, remarkably, happen. Everyone knows the world names. And breathes cleaner air because of them.

And then there are the others, around the world, nameless beyond their circle, numberless with ragged statistics, sisters as well as brothers it makes no difference. Beyond price to someone. Or maybe alone without encouraging weepers in the wings. With or without supporters they survive if they can, endure intact as long as endurance holds, approach the diminishing point, refuse to vanish, some shattered, all changed, impacting with the facts of the dark space below the pendulum—and crawling or limping away.

How it was with my father I could not even guess. Or I could sum it up by saying I did not know what he had become but noticed that his shoulder blades, too, were now sharper, more prominent. And his hair. I had expected worse and was braced to accept how it would be no matter what. Decently it was already growing back by the time he got to our oasis, fine burnished fuzz all over his head and I could look directly at him without flinching. Shivering a little but not flinching, remembering the great thing, a legend by now, how he had gotten hold of a razor after they had cut off his glory and reshaped it to regulations, a flat top slave crew; how he had finished the job in electrifying steel slashes of wordless defiance, his exposed scalp gleaming as ghostly bloodless and stark as a skull.

So that was it, how as a starter he had earned a black hole.

Wordless. Every protest he had made, for this or that, now and then, was wordless.

Or so they said.

And now he stood wordless, too. But with a difference. He did try to respond. With flung back recognition. Taking them all in. Eating what was served with measured caution, not ravenously.

* * *

It had been one sustaining goal, to go to Tranquilli's shore as soon as he got out. Breathing of space, confirming with eye the intricate and vivid details he had seen for so long on the inside of closed eyelids. Breathing the rippling heat off the dunes, hearing the cool wrath of the thundering waves, the soughing grief mad with the joy of sunlight shattered and scattered in spray.

To stand on the strand where they had sprinkled her as she had wished and as he had instructed, that had to

179

be the first free act. Before talks. Before any plans. Before this or that. Take off. Go. Alone. That was essential. Alone. But—almost. I breathed a deep sigh. He would take me.

*   *   *

We could hear the sea before we saw it, a rolling burdened murmur, heavy but somehow subdued, without (I realized later) the cry of birds. By contrast the air, the day itself seemed effervescent, bright and breezy, not oppressively hot. Fine. Tranquilli had always said her translation should be celebrated, no weeps please. The next dimension. All that. True, time had gone by but we would remember her at this moment, at this place, as she wished. In spite of all that still cried out of weeping and protest. Have it her way at least on this magic strand between the sky and earth, between the deep and the emerged. Was that unreasonable? As we pulled ankle deep through the sucking sand on the back of the last dune before the open shore, Mox stopped and said, "Sit down and wait. I'll call you."

I understood perfectly what he meant. He wanted, this first time, to burst upon the sea alone, completely, come what may, in a way to meet—whatever was waiting. With a reach beyond inured patience, the inevitable, beyond tears, even pity, but needing to settle, to say. I understood what he meant but I also felt like a brilliant cockerpoo mut who has been trained on signal, lie down, roll over, heel, *sit!* I pouted on principle. Also to reassure him that even my knowing would not be intrusive. I took not so much as one more step but this special time, this exception, plopped down in a sitz right where I was.

He reappeared on the ridge sooner than I had expected. In a sheltered spot half way back down I was making fingered designs in the sand and also marvelling at the finer precise tracings made by long stalks of rooted beach grass bending and circling in the flowing wind. His body profile at the crest of the last cast-up wave of land was sharp and emphatic. "Stay back," he ordered, "do not come farther."

He had disappeared again over the edge. I sat stricken. I realized dumbly that his overall expression, his visible imprint against the sky had betrayed consternation. For a moment I had to sit tight, not really moving, to take it all in. Stay back? Do not come farther? Why? Had I come this far to be a sitting fool, a tool in a cheating mystery, the weak or incorrigibly immature one who could be spared only by a lie?

For one thing who had given me this consuming curiosity, not to be put down without haunting consequence?

I crawled on my stomach to the top of the sand ridge.

I peered over.

Looking outward to where sea met land.

* * *

For a moment I could not adjust my sights to what I saw. On a bright open day darkness smeared on earth-sea as with a devil's brush? Or was I seeing the aftermath of some unnatural smothering black storm?

181

Was the ocean sick and had it vomited corruption?

In that first moment I sensed and then sharply saw only violence against what was part of me, against the earth, against the sea. And of course, like a deadly net spread and spreading, against the creatures. The smell of marine death rolled up the hot hillock on the sea side only to be slapping back to source by the flow of untainted air from the land. I suppose my face was pale, my lips tight, my freckles staring. I could feel all that. I needed no trick mirror to tell me I was crawling from the inside out, that my neck showed pulsing because my heart was flopping around like the disoriented gull below me at the base of the barrier dune.

It came to me, a thought I could reach for. In a great storm I had heard it was sometimes a life-saving measure to pour oil on angry waters, calm the ship-smashing breakers, leash the fury. Although there was no storm in sight to explain what was clearly a disaster, I grasped at that. A life-saving thing that had somehow gotten out of hand? Was that it? Sinking in myself I knew it was not the answer. True the surf was, if not calmed, at least subdued, the ocean heaving as if bound down and mightily protesting, kicking out of its vitals far below but rising only with a long-drawn muted gurgle, playing out even as it made a viscous pass toward rushing in.

I looked for Mox. He appeared small, bent, far off, near what should be water's edge. His back was turned against me and the landward wall of low dunes in a posture almost as though he were hiding something that if it were seen right out, raw, it would divulge too much. To be borne, that is. He seemed to be laboring at something physical, stooped, half straightening up and moving, then crouched again. Somewhere along the way he had lost or cast off his shirt and his bare back looked strange and shiny as if streaked with liquid soot. His arms too, even at that distance, seemed dipped in the same inky film. His jeans when he straightened up appeared weighted with clinging muck below the knees but higher around his thighs and buttocks his pants appeared glued on, a fluid skin.

What should I do? I was bewildered as I had never been before. To go back, pretend I had not seen? No, that I could not sustain. And he would know how it was anyway. I found myself at the bottom of the dune face on the exposed shore side. Without being conscious of it I had slid down and the back of my bare legs stung from the scorching friction. I was still above the trouble zone at the base of the dune and had landed near the dying gull. What could I do? What was there to help? The bird struggled again to right herself as I came near. A strangely voiceless and feeble gesture toward renewed panic? Her feathers were stained and matted with a tar-like coating, her bill was gaping open as if stuck that way, one sign of advanced dehydration. I tried to say something soothing but heard my voice coming out as sobs.

To look at her with anger and pity was to vomit.

I did.

Or should I say pity and anger, putting the creature first, before my feelings?

Vomit I mean I did, that is.

Like the sea itself.

*   *   *

Now I felt more as if I could take it. Lean and desperate, active, far beyond my years. I would call, I would go to Mox. I picked my way forward as the spoilage closed in and finally seemed to surround me. Although the beach where I stood at first looked only marginally sullied, when I put a foot out to test the underfooting it sank as into a deceptive spongy morass and my whole foot to the ankle was smeared with jet slime. I hesitated. Could I go farther? I tried to pick out the ridged or more solid places, inching forward. For a moment I looked up and shielded my eyes from the strange brassy glitter off the sea; dead fish, belly up, floated on the long laboring swells that, underneath, must be waves. The stink of fish death and of mollusk and crustacean death, cloying like a bad chowder, smote me out of the hot flat desolation that extended farther than I dared look. And of course the birds, the winged ones. I didn't want to see and yet I had to. Some bivalves—mussels? clams?—caught my eye as a morbid diversion. They had floated to the surface in what must be tidal pools, emerged dead out of hiding, opened, the exposed fleshy hinge of life bathed in deep brown froth as they swayed back and forth in the lethal brew. The sandpipers, where were the sandpipers? I could see none, no fragile matchstick legs upended and sticking up out of the accumulated ridges of offal at what had to be tideline. They were too small to show? Plowed under, then, in the grand scale wasting, submerged, invisible, contributing to bulk ruin, lost to identity.

The proverbial sparrow had fallen but this time had not been seen?

Marked I think is the word.

This was tern time. Coming and going. I looked around with a certain coldness. The first one I saw in the offal mass, identifiable.

I saw it. If the eye of Being did not see it *I* saw it.

I took a deep breath. I felt a connection. I could not explain it. But I felt a connection.

I cared. And there was Caring.

Expansion.

Response.

I called to Mox knowing I was too far off to be heard.

He turned and saw me. Some other signal finer tuned than sound waves? I was not surprised. His face was red, strained appearing. He looked as I felt. He did not chide me. He knew, of course, my being there was inevitable and there was no use wasting breath. An impulse danced across the distance and I sensed, positively, he was glad I had responded, countering words. But he had to let go with a shouted caution, "Man-o'-war," his distant voice came back against the wind, "sting. Watch it."

Of course. That is what the gelatinous chunks were, slobbering in death. Jelly fish. Even, no doubt, a monstrous Portuguese Man-of-War run afoul and fouled in all its poisonous extensions. Could the dead or dying tentacles still sting?

I stood stock still, respecting the menace.

I deliberately looked for the birds, feeling my center of gravity tipping dangerously as I held too strained in my stance while visually sweeping the scene. I thrust a foot out to balance only to realize that I had sunk into a sticky slough on the opposite side. It did not matter. Nothing, actually, did. For nothing could help. Try to deterge them off as some well-meaning souls did in other disasters of this sort? Even if we could, which we couldn't, it would do no good except as it gave surcease to the outraged helpers. These birds would never fly again.

They were everywhere when I actually looked for specifics, terns or sea swallows as well as the usually omnipresent gulls. Some were caught in the water possibly because of the habit of plummeting straight down into the waves for a strike. Or at rest time just sitting there on rolling water. Whatever the reason bird carcasses as well as other diverse organic flotsam dotted the long swells that continued to disgorge a burden toward the shore. And on land! On a flat jutting rock, rare on these smooth sandy shores, a large gull had been washed up en toto, left high but not dry by the tide, his wings pasted immobile, his lifeless body smothered in a glistening drench of black crude. He was lucky. He was dead. It was the live but doomed ones, the half dead and hopeless, that wrenched attention up and down the beach. The very land seemed to be quivering with astonished anguish, wings beating but not lifting, strangled cries, a whispered hiss here, a clotted croak there. I felt sick again. I looked toward Mox for some word, some—well—whatever it took. I knew what he was doing. Stooping. Rising. Moving on. His hands down there, near the ground, busy.

I had known all along, avoiding it.

Why did I have to be told, plain out, before I got it?

If not in words, at least—well—*worse*—

I turned then, sick but with no time for sickness. Back. Toward the one who had come for me. Who was waiting for me. Who knew I would come? Over the edge, out of the sky, with stinging legs—

She was still there. Barely moving. But deceptive in her misery. It was a long time to starvation although birds starve sooner, quicker, than most other creatures when it's unavoidable.

She barely moved I say. But she was trembling aware. I asked her pardon. I told her I saw no other way. She seemed to agree. At least she showed no further sign of panic. The oil made her feathers, her head, her neck, slippery. My hands, I saw, would be stained as she was stained. Her pulse was weak but still detectable. I felt the flickering beat in her neck, the place. I grasped her gently but firmly, speaking sadly, not deceptively but at the same time kindly as if something valuable was not, perhaps, after all, who knows, totally lost. As she struggled weakly I hung on with persistence. When all else fails—mercy? I had heard that somewhere. Or was I making it up?

I felt her essence running out, up through my arm, issuing from my shoulder on the left side, flying free.

EIGHTEEN

INTERFACE

There is the time between, there are the places between, there is reality split along these lines and that. Some persons sit at the bottom of a pigeon-ledge alley surrounded by dwelling walls and deflected noise, wondering what a rain is good for aside from washing down the streets. They are focused in a space larger than their bodies, but not much. As large as sight, say, right where they are. Bits of paper drifting, discarded labels, dog doo, torn wrappings. And dust. Always forever the sifting silting dust—soiling and the stuff of soil? Another kind for another purpose, say, trying to reestablish itself over concrete? For there are those others who, caught even in a blind alley, see in their mind's eye what a line storm is, driving endless sheets of rain across land as rolling flat and vast as a sea, smelling the wet earth as if they were there. They are the gifted ones. For they are able to remember what they have never known.

Mox had his agenda but he was not telling anyone what it was just yet. In preparation for whatever he was going to have in mind he dropped his exhausted body down outdoors on the summit when he returned from our down trip to the shore. No way could I get him up even the three rungs to the first balcony of the tree pavilion in the aviary spread and, anyway, to what purpose? Even a spitting shower was not coming that night; it was clear and balmy with fragrance on the updraft from the lower slopes. True we had had to use the lift to get to the top, a concession to the load we carried on our minds. Few words had been exchanged on the way back except as to the details of honing toward home shelter, peddling route, things like that. Now we had made it, we were back, and I too felt like nothing but dropping. Merebalm from the sixth level, silvered but ageless, a man that no mountain should be without, brought an air mattress and he and Sortie and Sallie dragged Mox bodily into the shade even if it was already, almost, dusk. "The sun might shine in his eyes," someone said, "on a slant." Others came, a small gathering, and I told all, getting the ghastly out, the details, finding no substitute for the facts. To share copiously, to purge dubiously, to lay on them some of what I had no way of carrying alone. Sympathy was there aplenty but fragged in angry tatters like a security shawl torn to shreds in a good cause.

With one small space not touched. Beyond the birds I mean.

The crying place.

I wanted the crying place.

I was bereft.

*   *   *

Three weeks. That's how long it took for Mox to return to himself, or at least enough so we would recognize him. He had not been in a mere sleep although it looked like that at times. Something deep deep deeper than even deep med, that was plain. Coma? Almost, but with vital signs less alarming it was the verdict of those who had support maintenance. A garden variety stupor? Whatever it was don't disturb his travels in another dimension was the consensus. If he had departed this way it was because he needed to. Who were we to drag him back to daylight consciousness before he was ready for it?

When he finally sat up on a cloudy noon, blinking and draughting in air as if to inflate certain areas of neglected lung tissue, I sent a signal down the mountain for the support group. It's good, I thought, that we have a dim day with muted daylight like in a birth bower to receive him among us again. Besides he was smiling in a simple way like a newborn. Before the others arrived he told me "Thanks Titmouse for the beautiful shower." What was he talking about? I had to think back, thrilled that Titmouse wasn't dead. The pup tent. He must mean the pup tent. Or rather the lack of it. "You mean when I wouldn't let them cover you when the rain came down—" "In curtains against my ribs—" "I was afraid for your eyes but you had them closed," I apologized.

So I had been right after all. Although it didn't wake him up right then he recalled it detail for detail. It had happened during his long sleep when a twilight storm was muttering off in the distance and lightning was licking along the horizon beyond the blue gulf of distance

193

below us. "Leave him alone," I had said, "rain is exactly what he is dying for. Besides it might wake him up."

When he finally did come to and was up on his feet he was ready for food naturally, other than the liquid and mash he had been swallowing at intervals on reflex. At first, though, he just stood there propped on a breeze, looking bemused. That means confused in an amused sort of way.

"If you have to come back—" he said.

He stood still then not only as if listening and looking but as if tasting and smelling, touching his own sentient borders. "A pivot," he finally conceded, "a starting place—" He paused, then, "not an end like you think, small one. But a place to start—"

"—start?"

He was stretching now with great deliberation. In the west the clouds were doing something queer, a narrow band parting, a mere quicksilver sliver for a peep opening into—what?

"Y'know Mini," his voice was stronger now, "it comes to me we need a new language."

I brightened up. "We're working on it," I told him.

"Sure. Sure," he challenged me, "Turning around old words. Making them behave. But new ones—"

"For things never yet said?"

"Something like that."

"Words not even born yet?"

He looked at me quizzically. "A start in the shape of an end?" He said it in the shape of a question but he was telling not asking. "That's important," he went on, "that the shape be—"

I just stared.

"—in turn that means an end in the shape of—" Was he getting hold of something?

"Not The Way Things Are," I put in for no reason except I sensed that's what he wanted to hear.

"That's the point, no. But reality."

"Not just any old reality," I heard myself persisting.

"No. But the real."

"The real real."

"The real real."

*　*　*

Mox would soon be on his way. In fact he was already on the way. Hadn't he made it clear that for him we were a stopping place, not a staying place? His decision, if that's what it was, had long been made, maybe back in the cage, although the full thing had not emerged into detail until—when? "All along. All along," he was almost impatient, "I've known it all along. But it grows until it comes to a point that says this is the day and that's it—"

There was a long pause. "It came together, sharp, at the shore," he went on, "soon. Start out. To go to—" He waved his hand vaguely toward the west in a sweeping arc that took in north and south as well, "them."

A chilling thought held me. "Them?"

I remembered once he had said that if he ever decided

to end it the thing would be unspectacular, like a whisper. He would simply walk west until he dropped, going out on the path of the sinking sun. But no. This was different. He looked almost happy, excited.

"Them?" I persisted, "who's them?"

"I don't know," he made no mystery of it, "but they are out there."

Again he made that sweeping gesture.

* * *

"The mightiest river is not the Amazon," Mox was saying, "it's the collective bloodstream. You get what I mean?"

He paused to let them try to take it in. Was he shivering? Certainly not. The effect must be the air moving below the threshold of a breeze. As for Mox he was sitting there among all in the world room, relaxed and smiling, offering to say the things that would explain or at least make some sense, or partially add up, the perceived reason for what he was about to do, at this stage, all that, before he left. A farewell of sorts. For me and all the others: for all the others and me. Around the circle, himself included.

Again he tried to say it. To reveal, not conceal.

"Don't get any false notions," he cautioned, "I don't mean what I seem to mean. No mere turnover of the same old scene. More like an emergence, standing on the interface instead of the barricades—"

Suddenly, with no warning, Mox put his head down between his knees and clamped his ears shut with his upper arms, squeezing his head in a vise of biceps, hands clasped forward and down in a straining knot. Was it a gesture of stated despair, mute but screaming? Or merely of frustration, massive abysmal frustration?

"When I say bloodstream I mean the exact physical thing," his voice came up muffled from the depths, "no symbol even. Cell to cell intelligence. Immersion in the reality that is smarter than we are—"

Attention was focused, swirling downward and forward.

"I should explain to you," it was a relief to hear Mox's ordinary voice. He was looking up from his tortuous squat, "I have this thing—"

Deliberately, then, he untangled himself from his own collapse and sat, once more, relaxed on the bench.

"An overcast? No. Not as confusing as physical double vision. More like between the layers of—well—more like an *under*cast? You could say so. In situ? Hm-m—"

He paused then to take inventory of what he meant. He too was puzzled?

"There whether I perceive it or not," he went on cautiously, feeling his way, "Not dependent on me. Not our construction I mean. Not the category of illusion either. No way. But the nature—the nature— You get what I mean?"

They were trying, Some were bent forward, empathetically strained and all or almost all had creased brows. Except Him and Her, our pair of bland-faced donkeys bedded down near one wall. And of course Greatfeller crouched among us who was making responsive chirring noises.

197

"Don't pay attention to my words," Mox tried to help, "just take what I mean."

He went on then with a different set of images. "Have you ever seen wild horses?" he started hopefully, "You know. I mean you can be only an inch from deliverance but see only solid walls, bound in less by what's real than the way you see it. The way a wild horse stays put y'know in a makeshift corral bounded by packing crate barriers, pacing and rearing and circling but for all his kicking never once touching the solid-looking fraudulent borders. *You get what I mean?*"

Whether they did or not no longer seemed to matter. Something was coming through. That was the important thing. *What* would follow at its own pace, naturally. Maybe something even Mox himself didn't expect?

"One thing I want to say is we might as well hang on," he hung on, "makes more sense—"

They clapped. Loud. A few whistled. A visiting Turk shouted something three times that sounded like a huzzah in his own language, high-pitched, resounding. Then they clapped for him in turn, crescendo.

"Who wants a flabbergast?" asked Apple.

"A full blown one," said someone else.

"Global in scope yet."

"Totally local too don't forget."

"—starting with septic window boxes?"

Z.Z., Zaptiah Zedd, on a visit to study our bloomin' biodynamic gardening, was on his feet to claim if not the last word at least one sliced in, "Like the time they drained the Hoaconougha dam before it burst. It can be done you

198

know. Disaster averted. But that's beside the point. Which is: reliably amazing. Muck flats exposed? That's what you'd predict eh? So be it. A wasteland the size and shape of the late reservoir? Hardly. A few weeks exposed and already a forest of cottonwoods. Six centimeters high. But a forest. Acres of twinkling leaves. Plantain too of course and the rest of the tribe you'd expect. Plus humming insects and stranded freshwater shells. But cottonwoods. Embryo saplings."

"Little trees," it was Apple again, her head draped in dream cloth, "I know some little people who could live there—"

But Mox was not through. "You hear all this about breakthroughs. Bang. Does it really happen that way? Spectacular. Recognized. All that. Hailed. Accepted. One big genius accepting honors. People. Look again. A movement is a movement moving because something has moved before unseen. But washing against knowing like a stream? The knowing that is in us all surfacing because the time has come. Like, say, the awareness that is in a bean, remember? Bursting to tell the hands that gathered? Way back. You know. Maize. Squash. Bean. In the ancient days of the Turtle Mound when the Three Sisters that crystal day among them together received the world-changing message, for a certainty, of the secret of seed—"

NINETEEN

THE ROCK

When Mox was ready to leave Heyzoos came up with all his pockets bulging with seed, an Andean felt hat on his head and a raw wool rhuana over one shoulder for general help, who knows what. "I am going with him to the end of the path to the zoo," he explained, "hand in hand. Then he will go north along the meridian, adios, and I will part and turn and go south."

We all knew what he meant. To get back to the squatter barrio high above Bogotá he now had an obsession. Still painfully thin but taller, still with enormous hungry eyes but a body that was tough with a stubborn toughness of endurance if not of muscle, we knew from the start that there would be no turning him back once he saw his way clear.

Three months earlier it had started. "My maMA!" he had suddenly burst out at a community council circle in the world room. His appeal spilled out with such agitation that all other concerns had to be shelved to help him through what appeared to be the onset of a personal crisis. His voice had had an almost keening edge as he cried

203

out his revelation with something of chagrined glee, something of sad joy. Too late? "Why didn't I see it when I was still with them, a starving bébé? Was my brain so damaged from her weak milk and my guts—my poor precious bleeding baby guts—so riddled from worms that it has taken me all this time to at last bust through to the truth?"

Heyzoos had everyone's attention. "The rock," he went on, his eyes ecstatic, "it is not the rock that needs to be moved like we thought but the shack. It is not the rock that is the bandit stealing life space but the shack. If we put the shack on the rock we double the moxie. Under the shack that doesn't sink for a change on one side we now get a runoff of catchwater in the rainy season instead of pooled mud under the sleeping shelf. But that's not all. By moving the shack we uncover soil popping to go. We plant our toes on earth and squish the warm soil. We have a place like everyone else for seed to split loose. Where the shack sat, hills of yams instead, a melon or two, who knows. I must go back, move the shack and uncover the lost garden!"

He was ready to start out that same night but was restrained with spiced eggnog and pleas to make plans, at least look at a map.

"Stay," said Apple, "stay." She was pouting, distressed, suddenly on the verge. "Stay! It's not fair. They are all gone by now. They said to you leave. *Stay.*"

But Luz shook her head. She turned away and circled and returned. She didn't have to say it, to point out once again the peculiar properties of the open arch we had in place of a door as entrance to our mountain, our refuge: if you are welcome to come in you are also free to go out. Would he take a bicycle or at least a skateboard, she asked, and everybody laughed, tension shattered.

But Heyzoos remained serious. After thought, the bicycle, no. If someone stole it along the way he would feel bereft. Furious, actually. He would need all his strength for other things than to get mad. Better take nothing stealable, not even the skateboard which would be a drag crossing fields. True it would take longer to walk 3000 miles than to roll or slide part of the way but there would be people and animals along the way and his own feet he could trust. What of food, what of shelter, what of national borders, worst of all the intimidating haute fortified barrier of the Panama canal? All of that, he said, would be taken care of when he arrived at each conundrum in turn. Why worry? "They will all help me," he declared, waving his hands, "I will show them they have nothing to fear. I have the friend inside who goes with me who is smarter than I am, a sharp guy, believe me. For food I can forage or beg or do a small job. A tree is for shelter, squirrels and woodchucks are campesinos, the stars are a guide and the air is the breath of God. What then shall I lack except people? Those I will hail as they come and if someone offers me a ride, a dry place, a meal, why should I refuse? I am only a rabbit nibbling or a robin gobbling a gooseberry along the route of migration, taking what's meant for me. In the meantime every step carries me closer to my brave mama and the little ones. O! How many new ones will there be by now?

True, papa deserted out of kindness so as not to make another baby but who knows how those things go?"

His mother? How could we shatter him by pointing out the obvious, that after all this time Mamacita was probably dead, the little ones trampled under by events, scattered, gone too? "If she's dead, the little ones too," he went on, "I will consult with their ghosts. They will know I have returned. Take my word," now his eyes were flashing, shining, "I will show them I have not stumbled at last in returning. The big thing is the glad news I bring back. If others are there in their place others, then, will eat for them out of the garden. My mother, my brothers, my sisters. Take my word. Have no fear. The mountain will bloom, the mountain will sparkle with stars come down!"

Of course this rock business was nothing new. We had all long heard about it, a heavy tale, from Luz Marina who had rescued Heyzoos from the clutches of la policía on the city streets by letting him hide in the folds of her voluminous skirt. Just one incident on her world trip to see how the children everywhere were doing. She had found him, a wild street boy among wild street boys, a gamin among five thousand gamins, with a singsong begging voice and sleight of hands, both of them.

It is true that, bone-skinny and shaking, he had clung on so weasel tight under her skirt that she could not dislodge him until they both got back, bulging all the long way back Mount Heapmore, when they both plunged into our spring pool as a single unit, coming up—at last!— with two separate heads bobbing? That, Luz said, was apocryphal. No, they had done everything as it should be done. At least they had gone, that is, back to the swarming mountain barrio to see his mother for permission, finding her hacking away at the rock, the little ones set to watching the littler ones. Overjoyed to see him, she was equally overjoyed to see him go: "eat!" she had cried, "eat for all of us! You will grow strong, you will grow tall, my first one, my love! This is a sign! This is good! You will return one day to bring us all good! Go with God! Adios!"

Ah yes. The rock. Like none other on the mountain, shatterproof, weirdly resonant when struck with the sledge hammer, with vibrations trembling deep in the earth almost as of a great buried bell. It was that rock, that big strange reddish-brown pocked monster that had seemed to symbolize all their woe, a constant reminder that they were poor even among the poor, all but prone among the abject. For when the band of landless campesinos had first swarmed in with desperate bravado to take over one of the last sections of steep open land above the city, Mamacita and her brood, being without a man to rush in and stake his claim, had instead been pushed and shoved onto the worst small plot; worst because the boulder took up almost half the space that could have gone for some kind of food crop. Scrounging such cast-off materials as they could to make a shelter, there was barely growing room left, then, after the shack was up, except for beans along the edges of the plot, with one banana tree already rooted, praise the merciful Mother of God, on an opposite corner.

Ah yes. The rock. Standing barefoot on the rock in her black skirt and sweater and howling imprications to the winds, some neighbors had taken pity on Mamacitta and the little ones; one man brought a sledge hammer on loan as a heavy tool worthy of the size of the problem and some other mothers brought their children for oversight during the day while they went out to scrounge for work or food, sharing a portion of whatever they brought back; on good days guaranteeing at least one meal, on bad days sharing their want. Lifting that heavy sledge day after day to try to break up the rock, watchful and straining because of all of the children, is it any wonder her last baby was born dead? Grief! And relief. Sad grieving relief for the small one beyond eye infections and dry fading hair, a mouth gaping for food.

Where was mercy when mercy itself demanded its gift only through loss?

Would it have filled any bloated bellies of the children of planet Earth to know that the rock was the stuff of stars, as huge in the earth as if Pacha Mama herself were pregnant, a meteor out of antiquity, a rare bolide fragment of the heavens, impacted ages ago and buried as deep as an elusive but still resonating dream?

TWENTY

THE LIFE NET

Was it a whisper out of daylight remembered deep in a dream? Dryads. Naiads. Transparent in light. Unseen. There. Companion of winds and uncontained water in any guise. What had the seed held back? That which could never be learned aparting, aparting. That which defied them all, the way they had gone. That which despaired of, said wasn't there. Ignored. Then forgot.

But to forget is not to achieve oblivion if that was their goal.

To forget is to bury, a very different thing.

For a seed to be buried in the deep is—?

What had the seed held back? Something elusive to force, intact, as real as suasion between this and that, so called up and down, over and under as our kind perceives it, the well known much touted light and dark. And we? Seeing in bits and pieces, splinters separated from splinters, unable to read the message of the web beyond the obvious (orb spider spangled greetings!), the adhesion of worlds noted in notebooks, equations sought—

"Why?!"

With a jolt I came awake in the straw beside the plump donkey pair where I had retreated to catch a wink. Was I hearing words in a dream or was it a familiar voice? High over head.

Mox was still saying something out there? *Up* there? Of one thing be sure. That's all I remember he said for sure. Of one thing be sure.

It was that same night, that last time, deep night in the world room and Mox was high above on a wire walking between banks of swaying air, the balance pole tilting, I below distance-diminished, a small strained face looking up, arms out reiterating the tremors of the pole, prepared to throw my body as a buffer against a fall.

The others had gone, all of them, but there were people there. Different ones, the night people, the street people who came in now and then through the perpetually open opening to get a snatch of rest, a warm dry place against a wall. The grey race of all shades, the gaunt ones, restless, submerged, never quite surfacing. Men mostly, tonight only a few but this time with one girl-woman who placed herself a distance from the rest. A teenage prostitute it turned out who had already had it but who couldn't go home. I remember because she was the only one who wasn't asleep or seemed alert enough to be watching Mox.

"Why does he *do* it?" she protested. A frizz blond, very delicate, hardly taller than I was, with a sling bag that came down to her boots and from which she drew, of all things, a ripe pomegranate.

"Your name is Vita," I told her without asking, "I saw it on your forehead."

She looked at me, an astonished blank. "I started Velma. But I got rid of that. Gita. Gita not Vita. You've got it wrong. Gita."

"Gita Vita," I said, "what's the difference."

She spit a mouthful of scarlet pomegranate seeds out onto the stone floor as if, for no clear reason, preparing to choke.

"Heh! This is not a public street!"

"It isn't? Are you sure?" She accepted the reprimand doubtfully with a pixie grimace.

I looked around then to be sure: actually it was public and I knew it. In a big open way never to be shut. Like the outdoors except for the advantage of shelter in stormy weather. Open, perpetually open, no shut-outs. Private only through familiarity, through belonging, adhesion to place not by means of containing walls and shut gates but by adherence to some central point that radiated outward from within. I stared into the drafty shadows, the shifting darkness, the sweep of overarching space, conscious of the one light focused on Mox, dim within enormity.

Gitavita did not offer to clean up the seed mess and I decided to forget it. What harm was it, a spongy little pile of gaudy kernels for the sparrows who sometimes invaded the world room for leavings and droppings.

"Crumby," she said with routine almost cheerful scorn, "a crumby audience. Look at them. Night crawlers. The

213

world from the underside. Why does he *do* it," again her gaze was high overhead on Mox, "risk his life for crumbs?"

"It's not them," I said, "exactly," wanting to tell it like it was without making Mox more of a hero or fool than he was, "not a performance. More like—"

"Practice then."

"No. Not practice. More—"

She looked at me incredulously, "You mean he's out just *taking a stroll?*"

Was that it?

That was it.

"That's it," I realized, "you've struck it."

"For real? A walk?"

"For real."

There was a slight noise. Mox was back at the near end platform and next he was swinging down the ladder rope, swaying. I ran toward him and Gitavita stepped back, fading for all I remember into the background, a mirror reflecting, the wall with ears, removed and indistinct.

Mox came straight to me with one arm out toward me. His face was glowing as he stooped down to my height as he used to do. His encircling arm, barely touching, was like a bulwark of flowing energy around me. I could feel it. The force of his being, low down to where we were, encircling, like knowing overflowing, uncontained.

"Mini! It's there. All around—"

He gathered me to him, his head below my heart, his faced buried.

Glory. I had become the crying place?

A source of springs.

Suddenly gushing from dry soil. Flowing. Not sad. But astonished. And flowing.

Freely.

Glory be.

* * *

The day was new, the light was clear, the breeze was fresh. We all broke fast with goat curd, buckwheats and golden treacle from the great old maple, survivor on the plain. The children ran and tumbled, shrieking, chanting at last a chant that paced their pace and finally reined them in to a manageable beat:

> *Mox, Mox*
> *strong as an ox*
> *shrewd as a fox*
> *Mox, Mox*
> *traveling Mox*

As for Mox himself he would go first to the Land of the Flint he told us, north in the territory of the Hau-do-no-sau-nee. From there he would wait for an opening, moving on when the time came, carrying or better yet tracing an invisible strand of the web that was already there, the network of a great life net!

But would the Ganiengahaga receive him, someone asked. Be cautious. Be sensitive. Be wise. Had they not fled to their inner place to repossess their own selves, to see again clearly the image life itself had given them according to original instructions? Without intrusion. Or co-optation. Hence distortion. And disruption. Finally possession.

True. Whether they received him was beside the point Mox pointed out. The point is they were part of the network, a moving fact greater than he was, greater than they. If it came to that he would lie on the earth of which we are all, his ear to the ground. Then he reassured us with his own confidence. "Who will not receive me?" he asked, "for I shall come with an empty pack basket not a full one."

* * *

And so we saw them off, Heyzoos driven by a compulsion of love, and Mox the seeker, the tracer of the strands of an invisible web already in place. Both would start along the meridian, we understood that, one going south and circling east after west and one heading north but circling west after east.

TWENTY ONE
THE OWL'S BURDEN

All this I told to the owl way back then on that day on the summit when he had appeared out of the blue suddenly, darkly, like an omen. Words racing words, all this I poured out to the quivering shadow above me, sitting all drawn into myself below in the piny bower as I fled back into self to arrive, the long way round, to now.

His response?

A ruffling, a moan, and then his terrible distress cry.

This time I was prepared for it, vibrating with it, with purging comfort feeling that it expressed all I had left to say.

But the crucial question was not yet fully asked much less answered: why would the owl venture back to the people zone? In the whole of creation what could induce the great nocturnal creature to come flapping back in full daylight? Something far more portentous than any words of mine could encompass, something that of itself alone would warrant the desperate defiance of diurnal exposure?

I was not wrong. The owl's distress, it developed, was

219

allied to something so vast and permeating, something of such a scope that it had driven him back against instinct itself. All I had told him, he let me know, was but a painful granule of sand in the eye of a weeping world. Old Hera, he said, was in trouble. Deep. Unbelievable. Attacked by a spreading disease, sick, if not unto death, at least catastrophically imperiled at several link points.

Would he have ventured back to the people zone if it were not so, crossing against himself the line between night and day?

Her arteries and veins were already running with noxious poisons and even her tears, in some places, were dropping as acid rain on once benign mountain lakes, the source of springs, of pure beginnings, not spared. Worse, her great oceanic womb, the amniotic collect for continuing and sustaining life on earth, was becoming a noisome sink of contaminated fluid with some lifeforms already smothered. Even her breath, poor dear, normally so fresh, so fragrant, had turned foul over wide areas and—more ominous?—her rare ray-shield crown, her invisible aura far out in the stratosphere was eroding. Little by little. Inexorably. Irreversibly?

"Mother mother mother mine!" screamed the distraught bird, "how can I help you!"

Still fair, still beautiful, still bathed in cooling moon by night and quickened and warmed by loving sun by day, magna mater yet had suffered assaults as brutal, as callous of her sensibilities, as explicitly physical as rape, her flesh of nurturing soil gouged and torn and left exposed in naked outrage. Or despoiled in such a way that lesions developed on her surface, necrotic, the septic soil dead, all plant life killed within these sinks and sloughs, animals and humans alike menaced. Deserts increasing, green cover decreasing, where would the creatures go? And there was something else, silent, permeating, unseen, what did it mean? Freshwater fish with tumors, cicadas emerging from the earth after seventeen years with crippled wings. The stamen of the telltale spiderwort turned the color of the pale child's blood.

The color of the pale child's blood?

Against my backbone the trunk of the fir tree shivered—or was that slender pole of support but registering my own shivering? Or the owl's?

I looked overhead and, still there in the web of dim branches, I saw the circle of feathered fluff that was him from the down side up, visibly vibrating, his agitation conveyed along every bough.

Terricide?

Was that what he was telling me, an ear, a human ear?

Ah! Of all the creatures to whom the great mother had given birth all were a part, not apart, but one. Yes all but one flowed as she flowed, born of her womb, dying in her bosom, struggling, true, but never against their own life support. One, only one, capable of standing apart, imagining self above and outside, turning to rend, turning to overpower, to subdue, to conquer the vessel of life itself, a creation's own embodiment. Had she not labored for aeons to give birth to a triumph of joy and beauty as fair as dawn, a creature of light to share the glowing

221

consciousness of the whole, one of understanding as deep as her deeps are deep, of laughter as divine as tears and of tears as cleansing as laughter, one who was no alien to mercy, capable of new visions above predation, a familiar to the art of healing, above all a creature of tongues, creation itself no longer mute to express—to express—

What had gone wrong?

The owl looked down on me. I did not need to look up to feel his stare.

For a moment I sat stunned, again pulled into myself as if my whole body had caught its breath throughout every cell. What did he expect of me? I was part of them. I had a tongue. Therefore— Bird logic.

"You don't understand," I protested, precipitated as over a brink into the monstrous futility of it all, "nobody out there will listen to me. They would call me the least, believe me, the least among the least—"

"The least! The least!" he mimicked. I could feel his eyes flashing, "don't lift a hand. Just sit there and throw dust on your head—"

The least? Can a grain of sand hold back a breaking dam in a flood?

And there was something else: if you're going to be so daring as to walk a high wire it's got to be along a true line of solid suspension, however precarious. Surely the wise old bird knew *that*.

"They offered me the top up here with the birds," once more I protested, "not to be above all but because I'm with all. To show that even the smallest of the small is of the wholeness of the whole? A true honor. A beautiful thing. To guarantee that the top will always be harmless. In perpetuity yet. For celebrations only. Sunbaths, why not? Or gatherings. Communing, that is, with the source of all that is. At dusk or dawn to toe on universal center line, to balance along the balance beam that registers the trembling of stars. A place, I mean, to get in tune with the whole. Just to be. To be part of—"

"Being," completed the owl. His eyes were glistening?

O! I was not convincing him in the way I meant to convince. Instead, clearly, I was only convincing him of something that he wanted to be convinced of.

"If I should go down the middle of a street screaming," I screamed, "no one would listen! Except to lock me up—like—like—"

Suddenly I felt sick. No. Not that again. Tranquilli you shall yet be heard?

All the small ones?

The orphaned duckling on the winter shore?

My eyes were also glistening? No. I had to tell it like it was. How could I make the bird understand that there was no way to reach them out there—not enough of them—or in time? That a mere tongue was not enough—or even flashing lights and a wailing siren? "They're locked in," I said putting down hope, "locked in. From the top. From the bottom. Even around the middle with a heavy girdle. Locked in—"

The enveloping silence was hollow. It descended around me as with walls, sheltering only as retreat shelters defeat.

Could I let the owl be crushed? Just like that? The

specter of a thought crossed my mind: was his heroic foray going to end the way a broken wing ends flight? Because of me. Because, alive, I did not yet fully believe the implications of my own breathing? Because, breathing, I was already as good as—

——?

Brave creature, ready to risk all, could I send him away without hope? But hope, great green vibrant hope could never be on the basis of false expectations shored up on presumptions. To have life hope had to be on the basis of the real, however tenuous, however bypassed or overlooked its bearer seemed, customarily given no more weight than a grain of sand among the boulders.

But there. As real as a granule in the eye of a weeping world?

I inhaled sharply and held myself poised. For what?

Like a burning focus I could feel the owl's gaze on the top of my head, on that sensitive and still vulnerable spot that in newborns visibly pulses, the same that (some claim) is the narrow passage of flight of those about to die.

I breathed in a long draught of warm evergreen fragrance. For a moment silence continued to envelop me but now it was vibrant, expanding, and I was conscious of a dart of knowing that was felt as a glow along the intricate network of my nerves. My voice sounded usual to my own ears, calm, paced. "It's true," I assured him, "I can't do what I can't do but I can do what I can do—"

The owl shifted on his bough, tipping toward me in

224

order to look directly at me, his stare as enormous and luminous as sky and earth.

"The truth is," now I was little more than whispering, "the truth is I do have something. The truth is *I can speak bird*."

END OF BOOK ONE

More Resources From
New Society Publishers

To Order: send check or money order to New Society
Publishers, 4722 Baltimore Avenue, Philadelphia, PA
19143. For postage and handling: add $1.50 for the first
book and 40 cents for each additional book.

WE ARE ALL PART OF ONE ANOTHER: A BARBARA DEMING READER
edited with an introduction by Jane Meyerding
Foreword by Barbara Smith

Essays, speeches, letters, stories, poems by America's foremost writer on issues of women and peace, feminism and nonviolence, spanning four decades.

"Barbara Deming always challenges us to rise above easy answers about who we are. Her insight into the nature of political change and the needs of the human spirit makes hers a unique feminist voice which guides and inspires us in the struggle for a more humane world."

—Charlotte Bunch

"Her work continues to be life-sustaining, as necessary as breath to me. This new collection is indeed a treasure."

—Pam McAllister

320 pages. 1984.
Hardcover: $24.95
Paperback: $10.95

RAINBOWS NOT RADIATION!
 BANANAS NOT BOMBS!
GRAPES NOT GUNS!
 XYLOPHONES NOT X-TINCTION!

WATERMELONS NOT WAR! A SUPPORT BOOK FOR PARENTING IN THE NUCLEAR AGE

by Kate Cloud, Ellie Deegan, Alice Evans, Hayat Imam, and Barbara Signer; Afterword by Dr. Helen Caldicott.

Five mothers in the Boston area have been meeting regularly for four years, to give each other support, to demystify nuclear technology into terms parents, *and children*, can understand, to find ways of acting which will give their children a future. The result is *Watermelons not War! A Support Book for Parenting in the Nuclear Age.*

Articles describing this project appeared in *Ms. Magazine, Whole Life Times,* and *Sojourner.*

Large format. Beautifully illustrated. Annotated Bibliography.
160 pages. 1984.
Hardcover: $19.95
Paperback: $9.95

"This is the bravest book I have read since Jonathan Schell's FATE OF THE EARTH."

—Dr. Rollo May

DESPAIR AND PERSONAL POWER IN THE NUCLEAR AGE
by Joanna Rogers Macy

Despair and Personal Power in the Nuclear Age is the first major book to examine our psychological responses to planetary perils and to lay the theoretical foundations for an empowering, personally-centered approach to social change. Included are sections on awakening in the nuclear age, relating to children and young people, guided meditations, empowered rituals, and a special section on "Spiritual Exercises for a Time of Apocalypse." This book was described and excerpted in *New Age Journal* and *Fellowship Magazine*, recommended for public libraries by *Library Journal*, and selected for inclusion in the 1984 Women's Reading Program, General Board of Global Ministries, United Methodist Church.

200 pages. Appendices, resource lists, exercises. 1983.
Hardcover: $19.95
Paperback: $8.95

A SEX REVOLUTION
by Lois Waisbrooker

With an introduction "Women in the Lead: Waisbrooker's Way to Peace" by Pam McAllister, editor of *Reweaving the Web of Life: Feminism and Nonviolence.*

In her own day, Lois Waisbrooker was called "the Abraham Lincoln of women". A dynamic speaker and writer, anarchist, spiritualist, and feminist, she was threatened with imprisonment several times for advocating, "women's control over their own bodies".

In her novel *A Sex Revolution*, women demand control of the world for fifty years to see whether it leads to the abolition of war. The book is a strikingly contemporary condemnation of the masculine concept of "defense by the State" which has placed us on the brink of nuclear annihilation.

160 pages. 1985.
Hardcover: $19.95
Paperback: $6.95

REWEAVING THE WEB OF LIFE: FEMINISM AND NONVIOLENCE
edited by Pam McAllister

"...happens to be one of the most important books you'll ever read."

—*The Village Voice*

"Stressing the connection between patriarchy and war, sex and violence, this book shows that nonviolence can be an assertive, positive force. It's provocative reading for anyone interested in surviving and changing the nuclear age."

—*Ms. Magazine*

More than 50 contributors. Topics include: Women's History, Women and the Struggle Against Militarism, Violence and its Origins, Nonviolence and Women's Self-Defense. A richly varied collection of interviews, songs, poems, stories, provocative proposals, photographs.

Most often recommended book in the 1983 WIN MAGAZINE ANNUAL BOOK POLL

Annotated Bibliography. Index.
448 pages.
Hardcover: $19.95
Paperback: $10.95

"A hardy, [   ]   usan Griffin

OUR STU[   ]
Poems by Ellen Bass
Foreword by Florence Howe

"The poems are rich with natural images, sensual and pungent; rich too because they are powerfully rooted in a woman's body and love."

—Marge Piercy

"These poems are sustaining and important for they enhance our sense of life and its meaning, our hold on life. We must see that they reach many. For earthly, for beautiful, survival."

—Tillie Olsen

Ellen Bass won the Elliston Book Award for Poetry, and is co-editor of *No More Masks! An Anthology of Poems by Women* (Doubleday) and *I Never Told Anyone: Writings by Women Survivors of Child Sexual Abuse* (Harper & Row). Her poem "Our Stunning Harvest", which appeared in *Reweaving the Web of Life: Feminism and Nonviolence*, has been read and performed nation-wide by women and anti-nuclear activists.

112 pages. 1985.
Hardcover: $19.95
Paperback: $6.95

A special deluxe edition of *Our Stunning Harvest* is available from Moving Parts Press, 419A Maple Street, Santa Cruz, CA 95060.